THE

Sarah Siddons

AUDIO FILES

THEATER: THEORY/TEXT/PERFORMANCE
Series Editors: David Krasner and Rebecca Schneider
Founding Editor: Enoch Brater

Recent Titles:

THE

Sarah Siddons

AUDIO FILES

Romanticism and the Lost Voice

JUDITH PASCOE

THE UNIVERSITY OF MICHIGAN PRESS • ANN ARBOR

First paperback edition 2013
Copyright © by the University of Michigan 2011
All rights reserved
Published in the United States of America by
The University of Michigan Press
Printed and bound by CPI Group (UK) Ltd, Croydon, CR0 4YY

2016   2015   2014   2013   5   4   3   2

A CIP catalog record for this book is available from the British Library.

Library of Congress Cataloging-in-Publication Data

Pascoe, Judith
     The Sarah Siddons audio files : romanticism and the lost voice /
Judith Pascoe.
        p. cm. — (Theater: theory/text/performance)
     Includes bibliographical references and index.
     ISBN 978-0-472-11766-6 (cloth : alk. paper)
     1. Siddons, Sarah, 1755–1831—Performances.   2. Voices of famous
people.   3. Theater—England—History.   I. Title.
     PN2598.S5P35   2011
     792.02'8092—dc22   2010047513

ISBN 978-0-472-03569-4 (pbk. : alk. paper)

Excerpts from "Sarah Siddons, theatre voices and recorded memory" by Judith Pascoe
Shakespeare Survey, Volume 61: Shakespeare, Sound and Screen. Copyright © 2008
Cambridge University Press. Reprinted with permission.

Cover: Painting by Joshua Reynolds, *Sarah Siddons as the Tragic Muse* (1784;
altered detail of the original). Courtesy of the Huntington Library, Art Collections,
and Botanical Gardens, San Marino, California.

for

PERRY, EMMA, *&* MAISIE,

whose voices I like best

In periods like the late nineteenth century, and like our own, in which the technological imagination outruns technological development itself, new inventions have a way of seeming out of date, or used up, on their arrival, like a birthday present with which you have been secretly playing in advance.

—STEVEN CONNOR,
Dumbstruck: A Cultural History of Ventriloquism

Preface

The British romantics were the last generation to go unrecorded, and so they stand on the far side of a cultural divide. The Victorians left behind a vast archive of images and sound impressions that testify to how they looked and sounded, or rather, communicate the reassuring thought that how they looked and sounded has been preserved. But the romantics seem more remote. Only those who were born in the waning years of the period, or who lived long enough to reside among the ancients, lived long enough to hear a voice recording. Wordsworth, the rare long-lived romantic poet who made it to age eighty, would have had to push on for nearly three more decades in order to have his voice captured by Thomas Edison's phonograph.

Since most public figures in the eighteenth and early nineteenth centuries sat for portraits, we have a good idea of how the luminaries of the period looked, making the absence of a photographic record of the romantic period less alienating than the loss of the period's soundtrack. This absence of sound recording seems especially tantalizing when we think back upon those romantic period celebrities who were renowned for their vocal performances: barristers, preachers, singers, and, most especially, actors—the romantic theater was famous for its star performers. Sarah Siddons, who was widely considered to be the greatest actress of all time, who died in 1831, and who was never photographed, thrilled theater fans with a voice that was never recorded. Siddons's star turns seem especially ephemeral, carried out, as they were, just in advance of technological innovations that might have preserved them.

Siddons's contemporaries expressed regret at the inevitable decline and loss of her voice, a feeling of anticipatory bereavement that, one might assume, would not be experienced by subsequent theater fans who, in the aftermath of Edison's innovation, did not have to worry that a voice they heard in the theater might never be heard again. Siddons's fans worried in advance about the day when they would no longer be able to hear her declamations.

But they also carried her voice in their heads. When Thomas Sedgwick Whalley sent Anna Seward a copy of *The Castle of Montval* in advance of the play's staging at Drury Lane in 1799, he insisted that she read one part as if it were being spoken by Sarah Siddons, as "written for her manner of speaking and for her's alone."[1] Siddons had so imprinted her voice on the aural memories of her fans that it was easy for Seward to comply with this request. Given how many romantic listeners carried Siddons's voice in their heads, we might ask whether, as we might assume, the voice became less elusive in the aftermath of sound recording technology. Perhaps the technology created a nagging sense of duty to capture every sound event, just as in our own time the ubiquitousness of camcorders, camera phones, and iPods compels us to leave no birthday chorus or piano recital unrecorded. The ability to create a recording may have enhanced the sense of loss when one failed to do so.

I set out to discover how Sarah Siddons sounded and also to find out what it was like to listen in the decades just before it became possible to record a voice onto tinfoil or wax cylinder. That new technologies for preserving and transporting the voice were morphing and multiplying while I was working on this book enhanced my interest in this subject and infused my research with added poignancy. Over the span of time I spent thinking about Siddons's voice, digital audio players were popularized and miniaturized. Cell phones went from being status symbols ("Mr. Johnson, the board members are ready") to pablum conveyors ("I'm in the produce aisle"). Talking was replaced by texting and tweeting. Japanese pop stars—"vocaloids"—started being manufactured from computer animated voices, no human singers necessary. By hunting down traces of Siddons's voice, I sought to recover a lost vestige of romantic era theater history, but also to understand how recording technology has altered, and continues to alter, our relationship to the live human voice.

As a growing body of work in the field of performance studies insists that performance, by definition, resists documentation, theater historians (who always knew this, but who—happily—kept collecting evidence anyway) gaze uneasily at the dessicated playbills and costume remnants they use to access quicksilver performances that took place decades or centuries ago. Wanting to distance themselves from the field's antiquarian tendencies, they strive to unite old-school archival work with new-school performance theory, to pay their respects to both material specificity and epistemological uncertainty. My study contributes to this effort by resurrecting the surviving traces of Sarah Siddons's voice and considering them with the help of interpretive frameworks devised by sound historians and media theorists. The visual evidence provided by portraits, caricatures, photographs—the most reliable and abundant vestiges of the past—can be enhanced or countered by attention to the voice. By trying to hear voices that predate the advent of sound recording technology, we recover something of what it was like to sit in a theater and viscerally experience, not just see, a particular performance. Such an effort also forces us to keep in mind that the way audience members listen is the product of a particular place and time, that our own responses to voices are influenced by our confidence that they can be called up or downloaded at will.

Did people listen more ardently in the romantic period; did the advent of recording technology create a difference in the listening subject? These questions haunt the following pages. Perhaps Siddons's voice resisted fixity and neglect by taking up lodging in the memories of fans who could only imagine machine recording, and so harbored voices more carefully than we do. Some of these fans were romantic poets whose fascination with the voice and whose grappling with loss were not limited to theatrical settings. This book grew out of a curiosity about how Siddons sounded, but in seeking an explanation for the size and longevity of Siddons's fandom, I came to explore how a preoccupation with the voice suffused romantic era culture more generally, and how we, the romantics' descendants, differently experience the voice and its loss.

Acknowledgments

I am grateful to the American Council of Learned Societies for the fellowship that allowed me to finish this book and to the University of Iowa for granting me leave time and research support through the Arts and Humanities Initiative and the Obermann Center. I also thank Stuart Curran, Michael Macovski, Peter Manning, Esther Schor, and Garrett Stewart, all of whom wrote letters in support of my endeavors.

The Interlibrary Loan and Special Collections staff of the University of Iowa library sustained my work over the long haul. The Harvard Theatre Collection, the Houghton Library, the Folger Shakespeare Library, and the Chicago Public Library made it possible for me to seek out Siddons's voice in the surviving ephemera of her fans.

For the opportunity to voice my ideas about Sarah Siddons's voice, I am grateful to Mark Schoenfield, Jay Clayton, and Leah Marcus at Vanderbilt University; to Dino Felluga, organizer of the 2006 joint conference of the North American Society for the Study of Romanticism (NASSR) and the North American Victorian Studies Association (NAVSA); to Fran Botkin and Erin Goss, organizers of the 2007 International Conference on Romanticism; to Sarah Zimmerman and John Bugg, organizers of the "Romanticism's Cultures of Performance Colloquium" for the New York City Romanticism Group (NYCRG); to George Justice and Julie Melnyk at the University of Missouri; and to Hiroshi Sasagawa of the Japanese Association of English Romanticism (JAER).

Much of what I know about the voice I learned from the members of John Durham Peters's Obermann Center Symposium on the Voice (Corey Creekmur, Kembrew McLeod, Kitty Eberle, and, most especially, John Peters himself) and from Judy Leigh Johnson's "Voice for Actors" class. Thanks to all of these excellent teachers.

William Leith's *British Teeth*, a perfectly constructed book about failing structures, served as inspiration. Claire Sponsler's detailed explanation of what was most interesting about what I was trying to say (and how I might actually say it) made possible a crucial late-stage round of revision. I am grateful, as well, for the insightful readings provided by the manuscript's reviewers, Betsy Bolton and Mary Ann Smart, and for the support of Rebecca Schneider, coeditor of the Theater: Theory/Text/Performance series. LeAnn Fields, editor, Scott Ham, editorial associate, and Marcia LaBrenz, project manager, at the University of Michigan Press, ushered the manuscript into press with a minimum of fuss and a maximum of finesse. Thanks too are due to the copy editor, Carol Sickman-Garner.

Over many years and through many permutations, Sara Levine offered ideas, shaped sentences, and urged me on. For her artfulness and generosity, I say thank you many times over, in a loud and clear voice.

Contents

Contents

Chapter One

On Paddington Green in West London, near where the actress Sarah Siddons was buried in 1831, there stands a memorial statue erected in her honor (fig. 1). Sculpted by Leon Chavalliaud and unveiled by Henry Irving in 1897, the marble Siddons looks out over the Harrow Road at the point where drivers merge onto the Marylebone flyover in a blur of speeding cars and delivery vans. On the day I visited, several years ago, a trio of teenagers, sonically remote from both the traffic's hum and the statue's marmoreal stillness, cut across Paddington Green wielding a boom box as if it were a public address system. The pedestaled Siddons wore a toga and a noncommittal expression, her eyes focused on a point far above the candy wrappers piling up against her plinth.

No better way of forgetting something than by commemorating it,

Fig. 1. Siddons statue at Paddington Green, London.

someone once said, and no better way for a scholar to spend an afternoon than to seek out a resonant cemetery and snap photographs.[1] The graveyard visit was a pro forma attempt to reel in the distance separating Siddons's world (turn-of-the-nineteenth-century British theater) from my world (turn-of-the-twenty-first-century American academe). I sought, somehow, to diminish my sense of alienation from Siddons's fame, which was of the excessive nature now reserved for celebrity babies and feckless rich girls. If you read the diaries and letters of nearly any Siddons contemporary—the reminiscences of statesmen, poets, painters, hangers-on—you inevitably come across a breathless account of a Siddons sighting. Joseph Severn, the painter and Keats aide-de-camp, counted the near-death experience of being trampled by Siddons fans as a transformative moment. Having often heard of "the superb acting of Mrs. Siddons," according to William Sharp, the compiler of his letters, Severn pressed toward the overcrowded pit of the Drury Lane theater to see Siddons play Queen Katherine in *Henry VIII*.[2] When he stumbled and fell, he was knocked unconscious; by his own account, his inert body was "flattened out like a pancake," and the pancake was then lofted over playgoers' heads in an early instance of mosh pit transport (12). (Mob scenes, it should be noted, are as common in Siddons reminiscences as bowers are in Keats poems—Anna Seward, too, recalled "struggling through the terrible, fierce, maddening crowd into the pit.")[3] For three-quarters of an hour, Sharp writes, the concussed Severn "remained insensible, and scarcely shewed signs of life," until Mrs. Siddons stepped out on stage, whereupon he regained his senses and sat "as one entranced and conscious of some new and vital influence in his life." From that day, "when the power and magic of Art was borne in upon him," Severn resolved to live the life of an artist. Looking back decades later, he would recall "with vivid speech and gestures his emotions of that far-back night" (13).

Circling the Paddington Green memorial statue, I could summon none of the wonderment that Severn described. Even though I had written about Siddons and planned to write about Siddons again, I had no accurate sense of what Severn was going on about. Siddons's ability to evoke overheated responses formed the basis of her celebrity (fig. 2). The barrister Thomas Erskine complained that Siddons failed to garner the applause she deserved because her audiences were so gobsmacked by her acting.[4] Siddons's biographer details, at length, her fans' ululations: "I well remember, (how is it possible I should ever forget?) the *sobs*, the *shrieks*, among the tenderer part of her audiences; or those *tears*, which manhood, at first, struggled to suppress, but at length grew proud of indulging. We then, indeed, knew all the *luxury* of grief; but the nerves of many a gentle being gave way before the intensity of such appeals; and fainting fits long and frequently alarmed the decorum of the house, filled almost to suffocation."[5] Luxury of grief! If I was honest I would have to admit that on many, if not all, of those occasions when I watched a play being performed on stage, my emotional response was limited to a faint disappointment that it was not over at intermission. When Sarah Siddons played Lady Macbeth's sleepwalking scene for a benefit in 1812, four years before Severn's conversion experience, the ovation ended the play then and there. No Birnam Wood removing to Dunsinane, no revelation that Macduff was from his mother's womb untimely ripped, no final battle scene, no flourishing of Macbeth's severed head. The curtain went down after the sleepwalking scene, and when it rose again, Siddons delivered a farewell address. Her fans had achieved my dream of a drastically shortened play, but not because they were getting antsy and wanted to go home and check their e-mail. They weren't thinking of all the things they'd rather be doing than watching a woman wring her hands on stage. They were enthralled by seeing (not for the first time) Siddons pretend to wash her hands in a bold departure from theatrical tradition, since Mrs. Pritchard, the actress who had previously owned the role, played the scene while carrying a candle. They stopped the play with their applause because they didn't want their peak experience diluted by watching lesser actors perform lesser scenes, not because they were looking forward to eating frozen yogurt. Or at least that's how Siddons lore would have it. By 1867, an unsigned account in *Every Saturday* magazine was recalling that when Siddons rubbed her hands during her farewell performance, "the house shuddered with an ague fit of horror and of pity." And the "frantic and ungovernable" applause that followed her departure from the stage, the shouted requests that the performance might close—these were the responses of persons "dreading an anti-climax."[6]

Siddons fan hysteria was so extreme that it invited parody. After one Siddons performance, a waggish newspaper writer reported, "One hundred and nine ladies fainted! forty-six went into fits! and ninety-five

Fig. 2. John Boyne, *For the Benefit of Mrs. Siddons* (1787), © Trustees of the British Museum.

had strong hysterics!" The mock casualty count continued: "Fourteen children, five old women, a one-handed sailor, and six common-council men, were actually drowned in the inundation of tears that flowed from the galleries, the lattices, and boxes, to encrease the briny pond in the pit."[7] The line separating history and hyperbole grew indistinct. Decades after Siddons's death, Edmund Gosse earnestly claimed, "Her audiences lost all command over themselves, and sobbed, moaned, and even howled with emotion. She could sometimes scarcely be heard, so loud were the lamentations of the pit. . . . Fashionable doctors attended in the theater with the expectation of being amply occupied throughout the close of the performance."[8]

I walked around the Siddons statue a few more times, pausing to examine the face that peers out from behind the skirt of Siddons's Grecian drapery. The mask of tragedy recalled Joshua Reynolds's iconic 1784 portrait *Sarah Siddons as the Tragic Muse*, which served as a model for Chavalliaud's sculpture (fig. 3). In Reynolds's painting, Siddons, festooned in ropes of pearl and a copper-colored, satin-sheened dress, sits on a throne with the figures of tragedy and comedy looming out of the darkness over her shoulders. The painting was exhibited by Joshua

4

Fig. 3. Joshua Reynolds, *Sarah Siddons as the Tragic Muse* (1784), Courtesy of the Huntington Library, Art Collections, and Botanical Gardens, San Marino, California.

Reynolds in 1784, two years after Siddons made her second London debut. She had first appeared on the London stage in 1776, as David Garrick's protégé, but she met with weak reviews and was overshadowed by Garrick himself, who was bidding an attenuated farewell to the stage. When she reemerged on the Drury Lane stage, playing Isabella in *Isabella; or, The Fatal Marriage* in 1782, she awoke to find herself famous—after six years of waking to find herself semifamous in the provinces. The Reynolds painting became part of a proliferation of Siddons paintings and drawings, both hagiographic and demonic, that multiplied over the course of her subsequent three-decade career. More recently, it has become a totem of Siddons studies, inspiring a 1999 exhibition at the Getty Museum. The exhibition, in turn, generated a volume of essays devoted to Siddons and her portraits, and one of the exhibition's curators, Robyn Asleson, went on to edit a second volume of essays, *Notorious Muse* (2003), focusing more generally on the actress in British art and culture, but repeatedly and productively circling back to Siddons.

Asleson's two anthologies direct attention to Siddons's physical appearance, both because the lavishly illustrated volumes reproduce a panoply of Siddons portraits and caricatures and because they have led renowned theater historians to reassess several aspects of her visual presentation. In essays gathered in *Notorious Muse*, Aileen Ribeiro discusses Siddons's costuming, Frederick Burwick analyzes Siddons's use of gesture, Shearer West shows how Siddons got conflated with plastic works of art, and Joseph Roach reveals how Siddons's person became associated with images of sacral monarchy.[9] But even before Asleson's estimable anthologies made their way into print, Siddons scholars had been using Reynolds's portrait to highlight her formidable physical presence. Pat Rogers's influential 1991 essay, "'Towering Beyond Her Sex,'" ushered in a wave of Siddons scholarship that used Siddons portraiture (which is helpfully cataloged at the end of the Siddons entry in Philip H. Highfill's *Biographical Dictionary of Actors*) to discuss Siddons's stage persona.[10]

Standing in Paddington Green, looking up at the Siddons statue which was supposedly modeled after the iconic Reynolds portrait, I was not thinking about the visual turn of recent Siddons scholarship. It was only later that I began to consider how this emphasis dominates theater history in general, and also romantic studies, which has also taken a strong visual turn in recent years.[11] No, looking at the Siddons memorial, I was thinking only of the similarity of gesture between the Reynolds portrait and the statue. In both portrait and statue Siddons raises her left hand, signaling that she is about to speak.[12]

Many less flattering Siddons portraits, I began to recall, also depict the actress as if she is about to speak. A caricature dating from 1786 depicts her as "Queen Rant," glaring in profile with hair blown back as if by the force of her orations (fig. 4). In Thomas Rowlandson's drawing of Siddons rehearsing (fig. 5) and in a theatrical portrait from the *Attic Miscellany* (fig. 6), Siddons has one arm thrust out and the other placed before her bosom, in what was for her a favorite stance. In a painting of Siddons performing in the same play that poleaxed Severn, George Henry Harlow's *The Court for the Trial of Queen Katharine*, Siddons is poised in midspeech, her right arm thrust out in an accusatory gesture (fig. 7).

The memory of all those poised-to-speak Siddonses, and the silence of the statue amid the traffic noise of Paddington Green, suddenly underscored an obvious point: I had no idea how Siddons sounded. This explained why I could read about Joseph Severn's life-altering Siddons encounter without really understanding why he was so moved. Severn especially admired Siddons's portrayal of Queen Katherine's dying scene, in which she was "altogether changed from what she had been, save for that deep touching voice whose tones, whether loud and impassioned or soft and pathetic, were like the finest music." Siddons's voice, according to Severn, "thrilled the air with melodious tones, and at the same time touched the heart with such deep pathos that the audience seemed to think it a merit to shed tears and thus appropriately accompany such sublime acting" (qtd. in Sharp, 14n). I had no way of apprehending how Siddons's "deep touching voice" sounded, since I would never hear Siddons speak.[13]

It was more than a little absurd that I stood in a cemetery in London thinking about how Siddons might have sounded, since, as a general rule, I was a notoriously bad listener who regularly finished sentences for my children. Once, while being interviewed on a radio show, I responded to everything the host said with the word "right." Right! . . . Right! . . . Right! I meant to communicate chummy agreement, but the word sounded like Khrushchev's shoe descending, like a peremptory attempt to hustle things along.

Fig. 4. "Queen Rant," detail of
"The Caricaturers Stock in Trade"
(1786), Courtesy of the Lewis
Walpole Library, Yale University.

Fig. 5. Thomas Rowlandson,
Mrs. Siddons, Old Kemble,
and Henderson, Rehearsing
in the Green Room (1789),
Courtesy of the Huntington
Library, Art Collections,
and Botanical Gardens, San
Marino, California.

Fig. 6. "How to harrow up
the Soul—Oh-h-h!" (1790),
TS 931.2F, Harvard Theatre
Collection, Houghton Library,
Harvard University.

Fig. 7. George Henry Harlow, *The Court for the Trial of Queen Katharine* (1817),
Walter Morrison Collection, Sudeley Castle, Winchcombe, Gloucestershire.

No matter. Right then and there, three miles from the Drury Lane theater where Severn saw Siddons perform, a stone's throw from the cemetery where Siddons is buried, within shouting distance of a woman sharing her sandwich with two mottled pigeons, directly below the Siddons memorial statue that was being passed daily by thousands of motorists, some obliviously honking—I resolved to discover how Sarah Siddons sounded.

Chapter Two

But instead I returned to Iowa and kept thinking about Siddons's voice in a distracted and unproductive way as I went about my daily business of teaching romantic poetry. The romantics were the last generation that went unrecorded, and so inspired a particular fascination with their voices. Henry James associated Siddons with a romantic past whose defining characteristic was its remoteness from an "age of newspapers and telegrams and photographs," that is, an age of recording media that promised to make the past less remote.[1] James was fascinated by the story of the Shelley collector Edward Silsbee, who sought out Claire Clairmont, a long-surviving member of the poet's coterie, as a means of providing himself with clues to how Shelley sounded. "Shelley had the voice of a child—high tenor from back of the head," Silsbee scribbled in his notes, underscoring delightedly, after one revealing interview with Clairmont.[2]

According to his contemporaries, Shelley's speaking voice, "a cracked soprano," was "intolerably shrill, harsh, and discordant," but when he read "he seemed then to have his voice under perfect command."[3] He was not the only romantic poet whose voice was an object of enduring interest.[4] Felicia Hemans claimed Wordsworth's recitations brought tears to her eyes: "His voice was something quite breeze-like in the soft gradations of its swells and falls."[5] Coleridge reportedly sang "Kubla Khan" so enchantingly that it "irradiate[d] and [brought] heaven and Elysian bowers" into Charles Lamb's parlor.[6]

The romantic poets were themselves fascinated with the voice and fretted over its ephemerality in their poems, perhaps because these poems often rolled off people's tongues. David Perkins notes that "in their daily lives the Romantics heard poetry more than most of us do" and that when they read silently, "they heard it more in the ear of the mind; and they heard it differently" (656). Perkins explains, "The Romantic style of performance made poetry a more sensuously appealing and a more emotional art than it now is" (666). To the extent that we imagine the sounds of poems when we read—and Perkins casts doubt on whether we do so at all—we conjure "a style of delivery quite different from that of the early nineteenth century" (665).

To Perkins's reminder of the romantics' particular attunement to the aural qualities of poetry, we might add a flurry of recent research that emphasizes the importance of sound and voice in romantic literature writ large. J. Jennifer Jones draws our attention to the importance of sound in Mary Shelley's *Frankenstein*, the ways in which the creature is thwarted as a speaker and enriched by his listening.[7] In D. L. Macdonald and Kathleen Scherf's introduction to John William Polidori's *Ernestus Berchtold*, they survey how the voice becomes an "appropriate symbol for the sorts of affection [romantic writers] are interested in, at once unusually intense and unusually introverted."[8] And Stephanie Kuduk Weiner points out that accounts of sounds and listening in John Clare's poems, as in romantic verse more generally, "enact an aural aesthetic that raises a series of questions—about sensation and knowledge, reality and representation, words and things—analogous to those raised by the discourse of vision."[9] Once you start looking for an aural aesthetic in romantic poetry, you find it everywhere—in Keats's "Ode to a Nightingale," of course, and Wordsworth's "On the Power of Sound," but also in Wordsworth's observation that Coleridge was "quite an epicure in sound," an apt description of the poet who used the phrase "noises in a swound" to characterize the sounds that haunt his Ancient Mariner. Susan Wolfson writes, "*swound* is a ghost of *sound*, a rhyme-word that lurks in the aural field without precipitating."[10]

Romantic poetry is full of the ghosts of sounds, and frequently dramatizes poets' efforts to capture or preserve them. As I stood in a classroom in Iowa, lecturing about romantic poets, I lingered longer than necessary over one such poem. In "The Solitary Reaper," Wordsworth tries to convey the melancholy song of a Scottish worker. "A voice so thrilling ne'er was heard, / In spring-time from the Cuckoo-bird," he writes.[11] Wordsworth makes the reaper's voice seem especially singular and alluring, but also, ultimately, elusive. "Will no one tell me what she sings?" Wordsworth's narrator cries peevishly, trying to fathom the song's history and meaning.

"Will no one tell me what she sings?" I intoned from the front of the classroom, sending my words out over a sea of reversed baseball caps, and then asking the caps to imagine why Wordsworth's narrator was distressed. "What's Wordsworth so worked up about?" I demanded as my students, recognizing a zealot, avoided eye contact.

"The Solitary Reaper" was composed after Dorothy and William Wordsworth saw reapers working in the Highlands, but it was inspired by Wordsworth reading a "beautiful sentence" in Thomas Wilkinson's *Tours to the British Mountains:* "Passed by a Female who was reaping alone, she sung in Erse as she bended over her sickle, the sweetest human voice I ever heard. Her strains were tenderly melancholy, and felt delicious long after they were heard no more."[12] Whether William and Dorothy ever themselves witnessed a solitary reaper is left unclear by Dorothy's note on their travels. She introduces a copy of William's poem by describing the "small companies of reapers" they had witnessed, and she goes on to write, "It is not uncommon in the more lonely parts of the Highlands to see a single person so employed."[13] Dorothy's observation makes the poem, hazily, the result of multiple possible sightings of single reapers and, more definitely, the result of her brother's reading of Wilkinson's narrative. This perhaps accounts for the sense of nostalgia that permeates the poem. Wordsworth tries to preserve a listening experience he never had, one made perfect by having never existed, or at least not for him.

My students clicked their pens closed, signaling that I was keeping them over time. As I stuffed lecture notes into my satchel, the instructor who taught the class after mine lowered the blackout shade and rearranged desks in a theatrically brisk manner, but I paid her no mind. And as I walked back to my office, past the low-wattage cabinet in which faculty book jackets fade and curl, I kept circling back to "The Solitary Reaper." Wordsworth's situation mirrored my own. His poem was trying to preserve a voice he'd never heard, and he was using a written account to discern how it sounded. I, too, wanted to reanimate a voice I'd never heard, and I had so far been using pictures as my chief means of accessing Siddons's performances. Some of these images, such as Henry Fuseli's oil painting *Lady Macbeth Seizing the Daggers*, capture Siddons in vivid freeze frame, providing something like live action footage, but they reveal nothing about her voice (fig. 8).

I was not the only one trying to figure out how the past sounded. Others had written at length about sounds from earlier time periods, and this society of retrospective listeners was regularly expanding. Alain Corbin had recaptured the cultural resonance of the village bells that punctuated life in nineteenth-century France, claiming that his history of village bells could allow one to "be privy to an auditory patrimony that serves as an index of a deeper mode of existence."[14] John M. Picker had re-created the soundscape of the British Victorian period, particularly the interplay between sound recording innovations and nineteenth-century literature. Picker argues that the development of Victorian self-awareness "was contingent on awareness of sonic environments," and that "to understand how Victorians saw themselves, we ought to understand how they heard themselves as well."[15] Mark M. Smith, in *Listening to Nineteenth-Century America*, claims that in order to understand the attitudes that led to the Civil War we need to consider the sounds and silences that antebellum Americans heard.[16] All three of these writers, in other words, suggest that modes of listening are intertwined with modes of self-identity, that in re-creating a past soundscape, we might re-create a way of being in the world.[17]

If I could figure out how Siddons sounded, I might also understand how people listened in the romantic period and how that style of listening influenced what they heard. At least two romanticists seemed to think that I (or any present-day listener) might be ideally suited for such a project. "Poems were indeed heard, overheard, misheard, and re-heard throughout the period in ways hard for us to imagine," write Maureen McLane and Celeste Langan, going on to speculate that "the ascendance of electronic media has retuned our ears, perhaps, to some aspects of the more orally/aurally saturated soundscapes we encounter in memoirs of the Romantic period."[18] They make this speculation in an interesting essay that depicts romantic poets as media-savvy denizens of a world in which letterpress printing was on the rise and silent reading was becoming newly normative. I wanted to believe that the ascendance of electronic media, which allows us to immerse ourselves in enthralling earbud-conveyed soundscapes, has retuned our

Fig. 8. Henry Fuseli, *Lady Macbeth Seizing the Daggers* (ca. 1812), The Tate Gallery/Digital Image © Tate, London 2009.

ears to some aspects of the more aurally saturated soundscapes of the romantic period, but I strongly suspected that it was the very ability of electronic media to preserve and replicate aural experience that created the divide between the romantics' listening experiences and our own.[19]

A century after Siddons's death, and a half decade after Edison's invention of the phonograph, Walter Benjamin, as part of his musings in "The Work of Art in the Age of Its Technological Reproducibility," associated mechanical reproduction with the stripping of the veil from an object, the destruction of an aura, "the unique apparition of a distance, however near it may be."[20] Benjamin maintained that the "uniqueness of a work of art is identical to its embeddedness in the context of tradition" (105), that its replication "substitutes a mass existence for a unique existence" (104). Siddons belonged to the last generation of actors whose voices were perceived as evanescent; this was a great career move on her part. The claims that she was the greatest actress of all time are impossible to verify; her performances survive mostly in the hagiographic accounts of her devoted fans, now pillowed in a nostalgic haze.[21] But that sense of nostalgia for something lost was endemic to romantic poets. Soon to be cast adrift by the subsequent history of recording technology, to be left on the far side of a great divide separating those whose faces would be photographed and recorded from those who would be forever lost to recording technologies, Wordsworth and his contemporaries seemed to worry in advance about the repercussions of these as-yet uninvented technologies.

Still perseverating over the changes Wordsworth worked on Wilkinson's stirring sentence, I couldn't help but dwell on the somber nature of his revision. Wilkinson claimed the tender and melancholy strains of the female singer "felt delicious long after they were heard no more." Wordsworth, half-borrowing, wrote, "The music in my heart I bore, / Long after it was heard no more." Wilkinson's line holds out the hope that the woman's voice could still be experienced in a visceral and satisfying way even after it was out of hearing range. Wordsworth's narrator claims that he carried the voice away, preserved in his heart, but as a burden, something he "bore," rather than sensually experienced. Wordsworth's poem stands as a record of the woman's voice, or the record of Wilkinson's record, but it also intimates that a record is a poor substitute for the original thrilling experience of hearing the woman's song.[22] Wordsworth's poem suggests that any record of the voice, even the one his narrator claims to hold in memory, would represent a diminishment.

Wordsworth wrote far in advance of the sound recording innovations of Thomas Edison, but not so far in advance of Edison's crucial precursors. The first decades of the nineteenth century represent a turning point in the history of recording technology since new ways of conceptualizing sensory perception made it possible to generate the earliest mechanical attempts to transport, amplify, and preserve visual or aural experience. Jonathan Crary suggests that a new observer took shape in Europe during the first decades of the nineteenth century. In advance of the development of photography, optical experience was abstracted and reconstructed by new forms of mass visual culture, such as the stereoscope. These devices, according to Crary, blurred the distinction between internal sensation and external signs, and made it possible to imagine the frozen and transportable image produced by photography.[23]

Crary's postulation of a new observer, one who was able to imagine the novel kinds of visual experience that photography unleashed, is matched by sound historians' identification of a new kind of listener who evolved decades in advance of, and served as a necessary precursor to, Edison's efforts to capture sound. John Durham Peters turns our attention to the long tradition of physiological investigation that understood the human nervous system as an extension of media. Peters writes, "To understand the origins, subsequent trajectory, and larger cultural significance of the recorded voice and assisted hearing, we should look not only to Edison . . . but also to the science of the sense organs that emerged a generation before Edison, and whose greatest representative was Hermann von Helmholtz (1821–1894)."[24] As Peters explains, Helmholtz showed that the diverse tone qualities of voices (and of all sounds, for that matter) derive from a combination of fundamental tones and harmonic upper partial tones, evident in the phenomenon of sympathetic vibration or resonance. This understanding made it possible to view all sounds as synthesizable; for Helmholtz, according to Peters, "sound is sound is sound," and the body organs that produce or perceive these sounds become the equivalent of other types of machines that could carry out the same tasks (184). Peters writes, "To fathom the voice in the age of its technical reproducibility, one must appreciate the ways that it was already externalized before it was mechanized" (179). Jonathan Sterne points to René-Théophile-Hyacinthe Laennec's 1816 discovery that a tube of rolled paper applied to the chest of a patient could amplify the sound of the heart as an early instance of "mediate auscultation," or listening to the body's internal workings through the means of an aid. Sterne argues that this development changes the relationship between a listening doctor and a patient's body, and also lays out the basic tenets of audile technique decades before they would be realized in the form of headphones.[25] In amplifying the beating of the heart, Laennec's cardboard tube stethoscope broadcast this sound from the exterior of its owner's chest. By conceptualizing the distinctive qualities of a particular voice as the product of a series of upper partials that could be reproduced by mechanical means, Helmholtz untethered the voice from the body to which it had always been bound.

"Every theory has its historical a priori," writes Friedrich A. Kittler, reminding us of how technology gets imagined far in advance of the moment when it actually comes to exist.[26] "In order for styles and works of art to even appear," Kittler writes, "epistemological knowledge must first have established the field of their colors and forms."[27] Kittler, Crary, Sterne, and Peters all cast backward to the span of years we call the romantic period in order to discover the moment when some not-yet-imagined mode of technology makes a preliminary, uncooked foray into the public sphere. We might read "The Solitary Reaper" as part of a larger culture whose concerns would make sound recording technology conceivable. Wordsworth's reaper is an inadvertent member of a corps of romantic era performers whose fragile and impermanent voices lent urgency to the task of devising mechanical means of recording sound. But Wordsworth's poem also wonders in advance, however obliquely, about what would be lost in the transition. Already in the early decades of the nineteenth century, when Siddons's voice was thrilling audiences, Wordsworth was fretting about the loss of the voice, but also worrying about the burden a voice might become if it could not be lost. Those who heard Siddons speak were already grappling with the issues that new recording technology would eventually bring to the fore.

Chapter Three

Who was the first actor to have his voice recorded? Perhaps it was Henry Irving, the actor who did the honors at the 1897 unveiling of Siddons's statue at Paddington Green. By 1897, Irving, who was born seven years after Siddons died in 1831, was an elderly thespian who probably took a personal interest in the way Siddons was being memorialized. "Methods of execution in art may vary from age to age," Irving intoned, "but in this monument you have a standard of conception which has made the name of Siddons imperishable." Noting that the monument was the first statue of an actor to be erected in London, Irving declared, "The work and influence of the actor are not quite ephemeral."[1] But the work and influence of Sarah Siddons *were* quite ephemeral when compared to the work and influence of Henry Irving, whose voice had already been recorded several times by the time he was asked to speak a few words about Siddons.

For years the only recording of Henry Irving known to survive was the first eleven and a half lines of *Richard III*, which Irving's grandson described as "all that remains of the living Henry Irving."[2] The material detritus of the dead Henry Irving—the malacca cane, for instance, which came to Irving from Garrick by way of Edmund Kean, or the green silk purse that was found in Kean's pocket after his death and that came to Irving by who knows what means—survived in abundance. But Laurence Irving implied that the recording held some essence of the living Irving that the boots he wore when he played Richard III didn't retain.

The question of whether a voice recording would hold more of the essence of the living Irving than Irving's boots was of immediate interest to me since I was drawn to the material remains of the romantic past like a moth to a flame. When I came upon the auction catalog for the sale of Siddons's possessions, I pored over the listing of the "Very Excellent Household Furniture, China, Glass and Plated Articles," and envisioned Siddons seated at her "knee-hole dressing table, with seven drawers, painted wainscot and ebony knobs," and surrounded by fire screens, foot ottomans, bisquet chimney ornaments, rosewood chairs, feather pillows, a brass fender, and a French fifteen-day clock.[3] I imagined Siddons barking her shins on the mahogany bedstep as she looked for a misplaced play script, or sitting on her spring-stuffed fanteul chair as she memorized lines. But if Irving's grandson was right, even the actual fanteul chair, as opposed to its paper auction trace, wouldn't be able to conjure the living Siddons as well as a voice recording could.

I lingered over Laurence Irving's comment on the superiority of voice recordings over material artifacts. Would the voice memo I made of my elderly neighbor singing "Love Lifted Me" when she was suffering from back pain, shingles, and cataracts, but still sang with full conviction, someday have more evocative power than the hooked rug she'd made and on which I stood whenever I did dishes? I wasn't so sure, but I spent a few minutes idly searching for my neighbor's voice file on my iPod, and then several minutes urgently toggling back and forth between the voice memos and the untitled song files with a rising worry that a certain family member, downloading Japanese pop music, may have eradicated her voice. Over a hundred years and many technological upgrades after Thomas Edison sought to "preserve for future generations the voices as well as the words of our Washingtons, our Lincolns, our Gladstones, etc., and to have them give us their 'greatest effort' in every town and hamlet in the country, upon our holidays," I had managed to preserve the voice as well as the words of an octogenarian Iowan, but she would not be able to give us her greatest effort on future holidays because she had been supplanted by J-pop.[4]

Edison expressed utter confidence in the phonograph's ability to replicate the voice faithfully—"It catches and reproduces the voice just as it is," he wrote—but, of course it was crucial to his enterprise that this seem to be the case.[5] Not everyone vouched for the faithfulness of the Irving sound recordings. Irving himself, anticipating the universal dissatisfaction experienced by people listening to their own voices on answering machines, responded to hearing himself for the first time by saying, "My God! Is that my voice?"[6] But in retrospect he thought fondly of the recording experience. Describing his phonograph encounter to the actress Ellen Terry, he enthused, "You speak into it and everything is recorded, voice, tone, intonation, everything. You turn a little wheel, and forth it comes, and can be repeated ten thousand times. Only fancy what this suggests. Wouldn't you like to have heard the voice of Shakespeare, or Jesus Christ?"[7]

Both Irving's and Terry's voices can be heard on the two-cassette collection *Great Historical Shakespeare Recordings*—but not very clearly. Irving's voice is trapped in a sludge of static, and even when I turned the volume up so high that the members of my household, both animal and human, emerged from their lairs to see what was going on, I still could not hear exactly what Irving was saying. "Now is the winter of our discontent," Irving declared. Without the text of *Richard III* in front of me I was able to understand no more of Irving's lines than I was able to understand of Death's speech in *The Seventh Seal* without the subtitles. No, it was worse than that, because when I watched Bengt Ekerow speak lines in a fitted cowl I could at least comprehend the Swedish-sounding nature of his words and the general comic ominousness of his presence, but when Henry Irving spoke the line "something something something something" with an overlay of mechanical crackle, he sounded like the voice in World War II newsreels. That is, my ear had been trained to associate static-obscured voices with images of American soldiers washing up on the shore at Normandy. Henry Irving sounded like Edward R. Murrow. The American actor who spoke Othello's lines just after the track in which Irving played Cardinal Woolsey sounded like Edward R. Murrow with a mouth full of marbles. After listening to a recording of the long-dead opera singer Adelina Patti, Wayne Koestenbaum wrote, "I wish I could say I heard the curtain rise to reveal Patti's voice in its original splendor. But I still heard the intervening ninety years, the curtain, the turntable, the hiss of reproduction. It sounded as if Adelina Patti were whispering something I could not understand, or as if the medium of reproduction itself were whispering instructions, codes, opacities."[8] When I listened to the primitive Irving recordings, I was mostly hearing machine interference.

Listening to Henry Irving, it was hard to tell why Henry James called his voice "wholly unavailable for purposes of declamation." "You can play hopscotch on one foot, but you cannot cut with one blade of a pair of scissors," James said, "and you cannot play Shakespeare by being simply picturesque."[9] However, the voice that got recorded was not the same one James criticized. Edison's emissary George Gouraud reported that when Irving strode up to the phonograph and began to talk, "it was not Irving in the least." "Absolutely he was frightened out of his own voice," Gouraud declared.[10] Years after the event, Irving's contemporary Joseph Hatton would recall that when Irving recorded the first verse of Monk Lewis's "The Maniac," his voice sounded "as if it might be proceeding through the bars of a dungeon."[11] The phonograph seems to have altered both the voice that spoke into the machine and the voice that flowed out of it.

The most admired voice in Edison's Library of Voices belonged to Sarah Bernhardt, not Henry Irving. Bernhardt, whose *"voix d'or"* thrilled theater audiences in the last decades of the nineteenth century, was the first actress after Siddons's death to challenge her claim to the title of Greatest Actress of All Time. I knew about the Bernhardt recordings because I had stumbled across a photograph of Bernhardt listening to her own voice in a collection of essays, nearly all of which make reference to Bernhardt's striking voice (fig. 9).[12] "The secret of that astounding utterance baffles the imagination," Lytton Strachey wrote, going on to say, "The words boomed and crashed with a superhuman resonance which shook the spirit of the hearer like a leaf in the wind."[13] Sigmund Freud, on hearing Bernhardt perform in Victorien Sardou's *Théodora*, claimed, "After the first words uttered in an intimate, endearing voice, I felt I had known her all my life."[14] The critic Desmond MacCarthy said simply, "She might have acted in the dark and held us."[15]

In the photograph of Sarah Bernhardt listening to a recording of her own voice, she seems just as enthralled as these fans. It was taken in the studio of Lieutenant Giovanni Bettini, who recorded Bernhardt's voice twice in the early 1890s (she had been recorded by Edison in 1880).[16] Bernhardt leans in to the horn of the phonograph, her face carefully calibrated to register rapt attention and surprise. According to a contemporary account of Bernhardt's second visit:

> The greatest actress on earth entered Lieutenant Bettini's room and quietly seated herself before the phonograph, which had been war-

Fig. 9. *Sarah Bernhardt Listening to Herself on Phonograph,*
© Bettmann/CORBIS.

ranted to repeat all the tones of her wonderful voice. "Recite something," invited the lieutenant, and Sarah broke forth into one of the
scolding scenes of "Frou Frou." When she had finished, the lieutenant set the machine going and every shade of Sarah's voice was
given perfectly. The artist was so pleased that she declared she
would own such a phonograph for the sake of hearing her own tones
as others heard them.[17]

What Bernhardt was hearing (assuming she *was* listening to something and not just pretending to do so) was not her voice as others heard it in packed theater houses, but, rather, a simulacrum created in a recording studio. "The studio was a necessary framing device for the performance of both performer and apparatus," Jonathan Sterne writes, adding, "The room isolated the performer from the outside world, while crude soundproofing and physical separation optimized the room to the needs of the tympanic machine and ensured the unity and distinctness of the sound event being produced for reproduction" (236–37). The goal was not necessarily mimetic art, Sterne points out; "it was about crafting a particular kind of listening experience," one that, in the case of Bernhardt, would showcase her voice without the distracting hubbub produced by creaking stage boards, echoing walls, and rustling audiences (242). Performers would stand before the horn of a phonograph and bellow their lines. As David Menefee writes, "High volumes of sound were required to force the recording diaphragm to vibrate sufficently to force the cutting stylus to make a good carving onto the blank wax cylinder."[18]

What the recording preserved was a studio session, rather than a theater performance. We can find a parallel to the Bernhardt recording session in theater portraits of the previous century, which seem to capture in freeze frame memorable moments on stage, but which actually record painters' reconceptions of such moments. In order to create a pleasing two-dimensional composition, painters would conflate two areas of the stage in their theatrical tableaux.[19] Eighteenth-century actors usually performed on the forestage, far in front of the sliding flats that were positioned behind the proscenium. Theater portraits presented a compressed version of what an audience observed, as if, in the famous long shot of the Emerald City viewed across the field of poppies in the film *The Wizard of Oz*, the green castle were suddenly trundled up into the middle of the flower bed. Edison and Bettini recorded not what a theater audience would hear, but what someone might hear if she stood a few inches away from an actor who was shouting in order to make sure he was "audible" to a machine.

Carol Ockman claims that without technologies like sound recording, we might not remember Bernhardt at all.[20] But does the advent of photography and sound recording explain why Sarah Bernhardt is still part of the cultural zeitgeist and Sarah Siddons—not so much? When my niece, another Sarah, was behaving histrionically as a child, her mother called her Sarah Bernhardt, not Sarah Siddons, even though my sister had never heard Bernhardt speak, or, possibly, even seen her photograph. I, on the other hand, had spent futile minutes staring at Bernhardt's photograph while listening to Bernhardt speak, because I had yoked the photograph of Bernhardt in Bettini's studio to a sound clip of an Edison recording culled from the Cylinder Preservation and Digitization Project at the University of California, Santa Barbara, so that I could listen to a recording Edison made of Bernhardt speaking lines from *Phèdre* while I looked at a photograph of Bernhardt listening (or pretending to listen) to a recording made by Bettini of Bernhardt speaking lines from a scolding scene in *Frou Frou*. However, Bernhardt's tremolo declarations and high-pitched quavery tones in the Edison recording only enhanced my acute sense of temporal distance. They didn't convey what Lytton Strachey or Sigmund Freud or Desmond MacCarthy experienced when they heard her perform. Or, rather, they may have captured what Strachey or Freud heard, but they couldn't account for those men's enthrallment by the sound of Bernhardt's voice. Even if I had a Siddons recording, I wouldn't automatically be able to replicate the experience of hearing her speak.

Henry Irving seemed to believe that some essence of Siddons had been preserved despite the lack of a recording that would permit her voice to be heard again. At the statue unveiling ceremony, he claimed that to certain characters in Shakespeare, "she gave a tradition which has not been effaced," suggesting that voice recording or no, her enactment of those characters still survived and influenced other performers.[21] Irving's words gave me hope that those voices that preceded modern recording technology could still live on, that there might be ways of hearing Siddons, and of approximating the romantic era listening experience, even in the absence of phonograph recordings. Siddons's voice had never been remastered or made available for download, but some traces of it remained, I would believe, and by piecing these traces together, I would find it.

Chapter Four

Early accounts of Sarah Siddons's voice survive chiefly in anecdotes of her childhood. We are told by her biographers that Siddons was given elocution and singing lessons from her mother, Sarah Ward Kemble, whose father had once managed a troupe of comedians in Warwickshire. Siddons's father, Roger Kemble, was a strolling player. Although neither parent wanted their children—twelve in all—to become actors, their offspring grew so "accustomed to theatrical joyousness" that the eventual stage careers of nearly all of them was an inevitability. Thomas Campbell writes, "The conversations—the readings—the books of the family—the learning of parts—the rehearsals at home—the gaiety diffused by the getting-up of comic characters before they are acted"—all predisposed them for the stage.[1] Siddons's voice showed early promise. A Mr. Evans of Pennant was rumored to have fallen in love after hearing Siddons sing the opera song "Sweet Robin" with "peculiarly fascinating effect" (Campbell, *Life of Mrs. Siddons*, 1: 47).

Siddons reportedly performed as Ariel in *The Tempest* at age thirteen, but she received her first big break as an actress after David Garrick got word of how she dazzled audiences at Cheltenham with her performance as Belvidera in *Venice Preserved*, a staple of the eighteenth-century theater repertory and a vehicle for ambitious female actors. When a nineteen-year-old Siddons performed Belvidera at Cheltenham she caused female audience members to fall to pieces. Aristocratic women who were preparing to mock the play's overwrought emotionality wound up weeping so hard they were unpresentable the next morning (Campbell, *Life of Mrs. Siddons*, 1: 57). Hearing this, David Garrick sent emissaries to see Siddons perform, and the scouting reports were positive enough for him to sign Siddons on for the 1775–76 season at Drury Lane, although Henry Bate called her voice "dissonant" and "grating," even as he recommended that Garrick hire her.[2]

Bate's glancing reference to Siddons's vocal problems sent me pawing through the kind of library books that haven't been checked out since before the library started using bar codes. I opened Naomi Royde-Smith's 1933 *The Private Life of Mrs. Siddons*, which purported to be "A Psychological Investigation," and which bore the tracery of an obscure institutional past, a bookplate with the logo of the "State University of Iowa" (an eagle wielding a bow and arrow) and a "Date Due" card warning scofflaws of a three-cents-per-day fine. The card provided a snapshot survey of Royde-Smith's sphere of influence, a flurry of check-out activity in the early forties, followed by decades of desuetude.

Royde-Smith drew on James Boaden, Siddons's contemporary and faithful chronicler, author of the *Memoirs of Mrs. Siddons* and also the *Memoirs of John Philip Kemble* and the *Life of Mrs. Jordan*, the latter two nearly as Siddons-obsessed as the former. Royde-Smith writes, "For James Boaden was *thinking* of Mrs. Siddons all the time, most of all when he was fighting his way through the hosts of other memories each memory of her called up." Long before Siddons was dead, Boaden "set about embalming his careful and enthusiastic notes of her performances in any and every book he happened to be writing."[3]

I dipped into Boaden's biographies with the single-mindedness of a grave robber, plucking out descriptions of actors' voices and ignoring the rest. Charles Lee Lewes spoke, I was delighted to note, "as a man walks who has a wooden leg, and every second word *stumped* upon the ear" (*Memoirs of Mrs. Siddons*, 1: 101). I seized upon Boaden's reference to the weak voice of the ingenue Mary Robinson, who elicited interest "from the peculiar expression of her face, rather than the tones of her voice" (1: 79–80), because I'd written about Robinson's career without once thinking about how she sounded. Boaden's descriptions of the "harsh" voice of Thomas Sheridan (1: 90), the "voice of *love*" associated with Spranger Barry (1: 90), and the "remarkably fine sonorous voice" of (the actor, not the poet) Alexander Pope (2: 49)—I copied them all down, along with Boaden's praise of Isabella Mattocks, who "was *not* the representative of elegance and beauty," but who spoke "with great point and vivacity, force and meaning" (1: 105). I knew little of Mattocks or where she stood in relation to Siddons, but was on surer footing when Boaden used Siddons as the gold standard against which to measure her female peers. "Mrs. Yates was majestic, Mrs. Crawford pathetic, Miss Younge enthusiastic; the voice of the first was melodious, that of the second harsh, that of the third tremulous," Boaden writes. But "so full a measure" of talents, as had been bestowed upon Siddons, "had never yet fallen to the lot of any one daughter of the stage" (1: 299).

For Boaden, Siddons's voice was a crucial component of her stage success, and he repeatedly describes how it transcended the voices of her peers. He writes, "The powers of her execution were in the volume of tone and the vigour of action greatly superior," especially in contrast to her brother John Philip Kemble, who "had constantly to struggle against a teasing irritation of the lungs, and to speak upon what may be called a safe scale of exertion." Siddons "was never balked by deficiency, she could always execute whatever she designed" (1: 221).

These written accounts raised several questions. Could descriptions like "remarkably fine" or "melodious" or "striking" give one an accurate sense of how someone's voice actually sounded? And wasn't I just rehashing Boaden's and Royde-Smith's labors? Royde-Smith gives thanks to a Mrs. Enthoven for being allowed "to examine her unique collection of playbills and press-cuttings relative to the professional careers of Mrs. Siddons and her family" (16–17). I knew no Mrs. Enthoven, with her firsthand knowledge of Siddons and her clippings file. I was sifting through the psychological study of a woman who had sifted through the biographies of a man who couldn't get Siddons out of his head.

Our inability to discern how Siddons sounded while playing Belvidera falls like a stage curtain between our critical responses to Siddons and the responses of her original handkerchief-twisting listeners. But dramatic performances are, of course, inherently ephemeral. Our lack of access to Siddons's early star turns is no more tragic or alienating than our inability to channel any number of other early stage performances, for instance, those of the young Shakespeare. But unlike the Renaissance theater milieu, which has been lovingly excavated and pored over by generations of drama specialists, the romantic theater has, until quite recently, inspired disinterest or even disdain in scholarly circles. One reason for this is the uneven nature of the romantic repertoire, a melange of Renaissance and eighteenth-century plays, edited to suit the proclivities of late eighteenth- and early nineteenth-century theatergoers. Siddons was famous for her Lady Macbeth, for her Constance (in *King John*), and for her Queen Katherine (in *Henry VIII*), but she was equally celebrated for non-Shakespearean roles in plays that are no longer in rotation. Fans loved her Belvidera performance in Thomas Otway's *Venice Preserved* (a play that was first staged in 1682), her Isabella performance in *Isabella; or, The Fatal Marriage* (the romantic era version of Thomas Southerne's 1694 *The Fatal Marriage; or, The Innocent Adultery*), her Jane Shore performance in Nicholas Rowe's *The Tragedy of Jane Shore* (which dated from 1714), and her Lady Randolph performance in John Home's *Douglas* (which debuted in 1756). Before embarking on my Siddons sojourn, I had never sought out, nor inadvertently stumbled upon, an opportunity to see any of these plays performed.

Alan S. Downer refers to eighteenth- and nineteenth-century theater as being characterized by "great actors rather than great plays," and Allardyce Nicoll suggests that weak plays were rescued by the declamations of talented actors.[4] Siddons's delivery transformed forgettable lines into something new and distinctive. "Mrs. Siddons's *Margaret of Anjou*," Campbell wrote, "persuaded half her spectators that Franklin's 'Earl of Warwick' was a noble poem." Campbell went on to write, "The reading man, who had seen the piece at night adorned by her acting, would, no doubt, next morning, on perusal, find that her performance alone had given splendour to the meter: but the unreading spectator would probably for ever consider 'The Earl of Warwick' a tragedy as good as any of Shakespeare's" (2: 5). It's no longer possible to be an unreading spectator of *The Earl of Warwick*; our only access to that obsolete play is through print.[5]

I was caught up in a larger dilemma, one that theater historians and performance theorists have been worrying about for years. Peggy Phelan gets to the heart of the problem when she writes, "Defined by its ephemeral nature, performance art cannot be documented (when it is, it turns into that document—a photograph, a stage design, a video tape—and ceases to be performance art)."[6] Phelan is not the only scholar to ponder the seemingly insurmountable difficulty of writing about a fleeting art form. Dennis Kennedy calls performance history "the act of calling up that which cannot be completely recalled, a conjuring trick practiced on the dead."[7] Jacky Bratton writes of the consciousness, "shared by even the most stubbornly myopic antiquarians, that our study is of something which is always-already irrecoverably lost."[8] And Joseph Roach points out that the "anecdote of irretrievable loss" has long served as a standard opening gambit for histories of the discipline of theater history. "This self-consciousness about the perceived contradiction of writing the history of so notoriously transient a form as theater," Roach goes on to say, "suggests a point of entrance for critical theory."[9]

The brash arrival of critical theory, wearing a garter belt and smoking Galoises, has provoked an identity crisis among theater historians, who, in recent years, have invested as much time in pondering how to write theater history as in actually writing theater history, and who have published their conflicted musings in essay collections like *Theorizing Practice: Redefining Theatre History* and *Interpreting the Theatrical Past: Essays in the Historiography of Performance*. You need only crack open *Interpreting the Theatrical Past* to get a sense of simmering professional anxieties come to full boil. The volume's editors, Thomas Postlewait and Bruce A. McConachie, describe the collection of essays as an effort to "apply new theoretical orientations to theatre studies," and to "move theatre studies forward."[10] And in "Theatre History as an Academic Discipline," R. W. Vince describes the "documentary imperative" that has dominated theater history as a discipline, and he criticizes this emphasis on the collection of facts because it "does not encourage the exercise of the imagination, the speculative interpretation of theatrical phenomena, or the aesthetic appreciation of the art of the theatre."[11] What Vince advocates instead is a form of "sciencing" (15–16).

Vince wants theater historians to distinguish between "hypotheses that explain a unique series of specific events and those admittedly fewer hypotheses that can be validated as generalized explanations in the scientific sense" (16), and he insists scholars must undertake empirical studies "within a rational conceptual framework that will promote an awareness of the theoretical bases and an understanding of the fundamental principles of the discipline we profess" (16). Vince asks theater historians to be both data collectors and theorists. He wants them to test an hypothesis "by applying it to a sequence of events from a different time and place" (15). However, as Vince acknowledges, actual scientists require massive data pools, while actual theater historians draw, by necessity, on the accumulated drip, drip, drip of half-evaporated and randomly preserved factoids.

Self-questioning theater historians like Vince are convinced that they need to go wide, to distinguish themselves from the leather-helmet-wearing theater historians of the past by hauling ass into the end zone and waving more generalized explanations in the air. I hoped to illuminate far-reaching issues ("to resurrect the lost voice of the period's greatest actress in order to chronicle the acoustic transformation of the late eighteenth- and early nineteenth-century theatergoing experience, and to explore the cultural ramifications of this change for both actors and audience members"), but in order to do so I needed to zero in on something more narrow and precise. I wanted to find out how Siddons sounded, and also why Robert K. Sarlós, when he listened to primitive recordings of great Hungarian actors, thought they "sounded ludicrously declamatory on first hearing" but, after three or four repetitions, felt them "chase chills" down his spine.[12]

Sarlós, a token throwback contributor to *Interpreting the Theatrical Past*, advocates a mode of theater reenactment that links him to the whole long history of fussy empirical fact-gathering from which many of the contributors back away.[13] Sarlós might as well join a troupe of morris dancers or swap hardtack recipes with Civil War buffs at the reenactment of Antietam—he is that close to losing credibility with the "new historian/theorists" who, according to Sue-Ellen Case, "no longer sound the old, wheezing one note of the seamless narrative style, nor . . . record the exploits of the unified subject, traveling the worn axis of bipolar oppositions in his quest to discover and dominate."[14] Instead, Case writes, they "play upon and are played upon by the keyboard of contiguities, microstrategies, and heterogeneous agents" (427). Pausing to consider the keyboard of contiguities, and wheezing softly, I imagined a smoky lounge where half-sloshed theater historians sang medleys, segueing from "New York, New York" into "Seasons of Love."

Sarlós knows his audience and waves off their objections. "Despite the condescension implied in the term 'museum piece,'" Sarlós writes, "what Shakespearean performer would not give an arm and a leg to be able to visit a theatre that, by means of ten or more generations of actors whose ancestors had worked alongside Burbage and Shakespeare (or Alleyn and Marlowe, for that matter), would present plays of that era in a meticulous, and ritually accurate, transmission of the original acting and staging style?" (202). Style is comprehended, according to Sarlós, in the "bits of apparently disconnected information that filter down to us regarding the spatial arrangement, the color, or the texture of scenic elements; the breathing technique, vocal inflection, eye movement, or deportment of actors" (201).

Sarlós's comments gave me hope that something of Siddons's vocal performance might have filtered down through history. Even if, as Peggy Phelan insists, "Performance's only life is in the present," the presentness of the present is often a pastiche of the past.[15] Joseph Roach believes that "the doomed search for originals by continuously auditioning stand-ins" is "the most important of the many meanings that users intend when they say the word *performance*."[16] And Marvin Carlson, making a similar point in *The Haunted Stage*, writes, "All theatre . . . is as a cultural activity deeply involved with memory and haunted by repetition. Moreover, as an ongoing social institution it almost invariably reinforces this involvement and haunting by bringing together on repeated occasions and in the same spaces the same bodies (onstage and in the audience) and the same physical material."[17] Carlson uses the term "ghosting" to indicate the process by which vestiges of past performances—memories of actors, roles, props, costumes, venues—come to haunt present ones. The process of ghosting was especially strong when Siddons was performing since, as Carlson notes, "For all of its passion for originality, the romantic theatre remained deeply involved with cultural memory for its subjects and theatrical memory for their enactment."[18] The recycling of stage "business," the prevalence of actor touring, the repetition of signature roles—all increased the likelihood that audience members would see an actor many times in the same role, in the same theater, or in the same costume.[19]

Might it be possible to get a better sense of how Siddons sounded by trying to re-create her breathing technique or her vocal inflections? Sarlós, Roach, and Carlson all seemed to think so, and so did other scholars. Jacky Bratton describes her attempt, along with Gilli Bush-Bailey and a group of theater students at Royal Holloway, University of London, to stage the 1817 Gothic melodrama *Camilla the Amazon*. The team tried to resurrect "a completely alien performance style," the gestural language of romantic era melodrama that was totally at odds with their training in a more "naturalistic" mode.[20] Bratton and company became convinced that the practical work of physically enacting the play allowed them to understand the forms of delight and recognition it unleashed on audience members.

Roach uses the phrase "kinesthetic nostalgia" as a name for the belief shared by eighteenth-century theatergoers that "movements and gestures descend like heirlooms through theatrical families."[21] Naomi Royde-Smith, in her sentimental recollections, manifests the kinesthetic nostalgia Roach describes. When Royde-Smith finished her research on Siddons, "when almost a hundred volumes had been searched and more than a hundred pictures and sketches had been looked at and put away," she turned to her memories of past theater performances. To Royde-Smith, the tears of Ellen Terry, an actress who performed decades after Siddons's death, seemed, as she sat remembering them, "clear and crystalline and adorable, as the tears of Mrs. Siddons's Desdemona and her Imogen must have been" (44). Perhaps Siddons lived on in a surviving actor's gestures or in a living actor's voice.[22] Perhaps if I could find a way to physically enact a Siddons performance, I might hear her speak again.

Chapter Five

If you are an undergraduate at a large Midwestern university in the United States and you sign up for a summer school class entitled "Voice for Actors," you will find yourself playing games designed to get you breathing hard. And if you are a middle-aged college professor auditing this class, not because you have theatrical aspirations but because you have embarked upon a misguided Stanislavskian attempt to imagine what it was like to be Sarah Siddons, you will find yourself staggering barefooted around a dance studio with budding thespians whose dodgeball skills have not atrophied nearly as badly as yours have. When, in the spare minutes before class begins, students discuss actors they admire, you mention Katharine Cornell, and it becomes immediately apparent that no one else has heard of Cornell, the American Sarah Siddons who toured provincial theaters during the Depression, mesmerizing audiences with her ardent gestures and piercing stare.[1] The class members are more conversant in the acting styles of Johnny Depp and Reese Witherspoon, movie stars who have not risked humiliation by performing on stage. No matter. The students are fleet of foot and precise of aim, and soon everyone is breathing so hard they can barely hear the instructor, who speaks with the perfect enunciation of a British news reader. Her first pronouncements: "Everything to do with the voice is housed inside the body," and "How you breathe is the furnace of your entire vocal capability."[2]

Siddons's vocal capability was called into question during her first ill-fated foray onto the London stage; in 1775 she played Portia in *The Merchant of Venice* and received anemic reviews. Siddons's Drury Lane debut coincided with David Garrick's retirement from the stage; his many final performances (his last Richard! his last Lear! his last Hamlet!) drew focus away from her first performances, but even if Garrick had not been bidding farewell at the precise moment when she was introducing herself to London audiences, her voice would have had difficulty rising over the din of more experienced actors in well-established roles. If you troll for Siddons mentions in the microfilm newspaper record of the 1775–76 London season, trying to find reports of her performances, you will be most impressed by what a small fish you are trying to hook in a sea of flashier theatrical fauna. Combing through the "Theatrical Intelligence" columns in the *Morning Post* and the *Morning Chronicle,* one can find the advertisement for the Drury Lane *Merchant of Venice* that identifies the actress playing Portia as "A Young Lady, first appearance." Unheralded, Siddons played the role several more times before retreating from the stage, only to make a few desultory reappearances, most unfortunately in the title role of *Epicoene,* a bit of miscasting that audiences resented, before playing Lady Anne in Garrick's final staging of *Richard III.*

One learns only a little about Siddons's stage presence by reading theater news published during her first season, but one learns a lot about the amount of attention that was devoted to actors' voices. A few days after Siddons's first appearance, a review of Thomas Sheridan's performance as *Hamlet* at Covent Garden took the actor to task for his vocal limitations. "In that wonderful soliloquy, which requires all the tuneful variations of the most musical and comprehensive voice," the reviewer wrote, "he gave us the whole, upon the only two notes he possesses, that of *C sharp* and *B flat*"; "this may produce an ideal harmony of oratory to an ear long accustomed to its tones, but an unprejudiced one must be tortured with the discord."[3] A day later, a reviewer for the same paper disparaged Sheridan's performance as Richard III and also singled out Mrs. Hunter for special opprobrium: "The tones of her voice were but ill adapted last night to the distress of the Queen."[4] Even when the paper's theater reviewer was pleased with a vocal performance—a novice actor named Webster was praised for having a voice that was "in general harmonious, varying, and powerful"—the reviewer offered the actor "a friendly intimation" regarding his vocal technique.

"We think he has a little guttural, a peculiarity, (perhaps acquired in singing,) in some of the lower tones of his voice, which sound affectedly and unpleasing," the reviewer noted, going on to warn, "An inattention to this error, may prove fatal to every excellence."[5]

I could sympathize with the guttural Webster, being possessed of a voice whose inadequacies were being underscored by my "Voice for Actors" class, but since no one has ever assumed that I should speak in harmonious tones, I have been able to go through life, stammering and braying and alienating all those who hear me without drawing particular attention to my vocal inadequacies. Webster and Siddons had more riding on their voices than do stage actors of our own day (who are often miked), let alone nasal-sounding, word-swallowing nonthespians like myself. The attention the reviewer focused on poor Webster's vocal idiosyncracies represents a mere sample of a larger eighteenth-century preoccupation with the art of speaking well. At the very moment when Siddons first spoke on the Drury Lane stage, several "elocutionists" were providing speaking tutorials to the public at large. The same Thomas Sheridan who was taking abuse from the theater critics published *A Course of Lectures on Elocution* in 1762, and followed this volume up with *Lectures on the Art of Reading* in 1775, the year of Siddons's debut, a year that also saw the publication of William Cockin's *The Art of Delivering Written Language*.[6] Sheridan insisted that elocution embody the whole person, that good speaking is an affair of the entire body. Just as "the human voice is furnished with an infinite variety of tones, suitable to the infinite variety of emotions in the mind," Sheridan wrote, "so are the human countenance and limbs, capable of an infinite variety of changes, suitable to the tones; or rather to the emotions, whence they both take their rise."[7]

It's possible that the role of Portia in *The Merchant of Venice* did not give Siddons's voice enough range to show what it could do. Boaden believed that Siddons was incapable of a small performance. He wrote of her performances, "They have one uniform character. There is no littleness, occasionally betraying the hesitation or lovely timidity of the sex" (*Memoirs of Mrs. Siddons*, 1: 221). Portia first appears in scene 2 of Act 1, a scene that chiefly serves to introduce the three-casket challenge that her father has devised as a means of testing her suitors. In Elizabeth Inchbald's edition of the play, Portia does not reappear on stage until scene 2 of Act 3 (when Bassanio undertakes the casket challenge and wins Portia by selecting the lead casket), but even if Garrick included the scenes Inchbald leaves out, the Portia depicted in those scenes is primarily a pawn of her father, forced to passively stand by as a series of suitors engage in a contest that will determine her future, over which she has no control.

In the second half of the play Portia assumes a more active role as she makes plans to disguise herself "and speak between the change of man and boy / With a reed voice." But if Siddons attempted to speak with an adolescent voice in a comic transformation, she would have been playing against type. Portia speaks the play's most famous words in Act 4, voicing in the guise of Doctor Balthazar the serious words that stand as an inspiring moral imperative: "The quality of mercy is not strained, / It droppeth as the gentle rain from heaven / Upon the place beneath." She gets the best lines, but they are quiet lines. This is still true in Act 5, when her ruse stands revealed. Before this occurs she comments, "That light we see is burning in my hall. / How far that little candle throws his beams! / So shines a good deed in a naughty world." The speeches do not call for emotional displays. Portia is calm and resolved, and while Siddons was good at conveying moral authority, she was even better at conveying extremes of emotion (or at evoking extremes of emotion from her audience). Of course, it's also possible that Siddons's perceived inadequacies resulted from inadequate voice control rather than poor role selection. Perhaps she needed a "Voice for Actors" class, and failing that, was doomed to speaking nervously on stage in a manner that made no grand impression.

"Voice for Actors" will not, as it turns out, turn anyone into a Sarah Siddons—at least not during the compressed three-week summer-school session—but it does lay out some terms that are useful in trying to figure out what theatrical intelligencers may have been trying to describe when they labeled a voice "harsh" or "melodious" or "varying" or "peculiar." These commentators tried to convey how voices uniquely resonated; that is, they described the results of a series of bodily processes instigated by the movement of air. This explains why a good voice teacher spends most of her time teaching people how to breathe. Untrained breathers are clavicular breathers who only take air into the upper portion of the lungs. In order to push air into the lower lungs, one has to breathe from the middle of the body, causing the diaphragm (a dome-shaped muscle that separates the thorax from the abdomen) to contract, and thus allowing the lower part of the lungs to inflate into this freed-up space. To speak "Now is the winter of our discontent / Made glorious summer by the son of York," you either have to have enough breath to get to the end of the sentence, or you have to expel enough breath in speaking the first line of the sentence to allow ample breath intake before the second line. When the nineteenth-century thespian Fred Belton, performing opposite the aging diva Charlotte Cushman, lost himself in an embrace, he was pulled back into the moment by Cushman hissing, "If you squeeze me so tight I shan't get breath for my next speech."[8]

Student actors learn how to fully inflate by lying on their backs and trying to make books rise and fall over their diaphragms. Edwardian actors (and possibly actors of Siddons's day) were schooled in the method of "rib reserve," a technique for preserving breath by keeping the ribs expanded with air while simultaneously taking diaphragm breaths. When the lower lung supply gets exhausted, the rib reservist uses the rest of the breath to get to the end of a line. The technique demanded an erect carriage that tended to make actors stand rather stiffly. Ian McKellen, who was taught this technique as a child, describes aching from his center through his shoulders and up to his ears as he strained to keep his ribcage hoisted.[9]

The history of vocal remediation is a history of instructors advocating naturalness even as they require students to hold their ribcages aloft. Sheridan insists that "the rule by which all public speakers are to guide themselves is obvious and easy": they are to "give up all pretensions to art, for it is certain that it is better to have none, than not enough" (120). In his *Lectures*, Sheridan veers constantly between an impulse to systematize speaking methods—he is especially critical of the lack of an established English school of elocution—and misgivings about the inherent artificiality of rote training. "Faults which come from constant habit," he writes, "have an ease with them which takes away their disagreeableness" (129). But he also recommends that Cockney speakers allot "a certain portion of time every day, to read aloud in the hearing of a friend, all words in the dictionary" beginning with v's and w's, sounds these speakers had a tendency to mispronounce (33).

Voice coaches seek to help students rely on their "natural voice," the voice with which we come into the world at birth, and the antidote to what Patsy Rodenburg, voice coach to the Royal Shakespeare Company, calls the "habitual voice," a voice "encrusted with restrictive tendencies that only awareness and exercise can undo and counteract."[10] Some voice specialists call the natural voice a "free" or "centered" voice; all potentiality, it stands ready to do its owner's bidding. When Siddons recited Portia's opening line ("By my troth, Nerissa, my little body is aweary of this great world"), or when she uttered the play's most famous speech ("The quality of mercy is not strained . . ."), she did so with a restricted or decentered voice. The *Morning Chronicle* reviewer commented, "We last night found her voice rather deficient in variety and clearness of tone; but this defect might be ascribable either to a cold, or to that want of collectedness which is ever discoverable on a first appearance in a Theatre Royal."[11] Another reviewer doubted her command of correct elocution, her ability to project "anything beyond mediocrity," given that "her voice (that requisite of all public speakers) is far from being favourable to her progress as an actress." This reviewer for the *Middlesex Journal* continued, "It is feared she possess a monotone not to be got rid of; there is also vulgarity in her tones, ill calculated to sustain that line in a theatre she has at first been held forth in."[12] A more kindly reviewer, writing for the *Morning Post*, made allowances for her "great natural diffidence," but conceded that "at times her voice was rather low," and that "her fears last night . . . prevented her from doing justice to her powers."[13]

In order to achieve the "free" voice that eluded her on opening night, Siddons would have needed to cultivate a particular kind of openness that optimizes the sound produced by breath blowing through the vibrating vocal folds. This sound is affected by the position of the soft palate, the lips, the tongue—all of the body parts that shape the resonating cavities of throat, mouth, and nose. Siddons apparently failed to achieve sufficient vocal variety, a product of pitch level, pace, phrasing, rhythm, emphasis, intonation patterns, and inflection. It's possible she was suffering from tongue root tension, which might have been remedied by doing lizard-like tongue thrusts before going on stage, or she might have been speaking with a tense pharynx, which she could have relaxed by speaking the line "Only Owen owns a gold rover," once with her tongue hanging out of her mouth, and once with her tongue tucked back in. She might have benefited from carrying out Patsy Rodenburg's Readiness to Speak exercises, which would have encouraged her to walk with energy and purpose, or to press her hands against a wall, or to lift a chair over her head—just before she strode out on stage and spoke her first lines. But even a Ready to Speak acolyte, a diligent student who has committed to memory one of Lady Macbeth's monologues and who has rehearsed that speech before a sniggering home audience, may find, when she performs before a dozen theater majors, that her fears prevent her from doing justice to her power.

Chapter Six

The whole-body approach to the voice espoused by Thomas Sheridan and my "Voice for Actors" teacher also survives in Roland Barthes's locution "the grain of the voice," which he defines as "the body in the singing voice," and as that something that comes directly from "the depths of the body's cavities, the muscles, the membranes, the cartilage."[1] Writers on the voice gesture toward Barthes in an inevitable, but often glancing way, registering familiarity with his voice/grain image—check!—while quickening their strides so as to avoid having anyone demand that they explain precisely what Barthes is trying to say. I hoped that Barthes's phrase would help me to understand how Siddons went from being a cast-off ingenue to being the enthralling actor who caused audience members to lose control of their faculties and who led Joseph Severn to pledge his troth to art.

The word "grain" conjures, for a literal-minded person who is having some flooring issues, the longitudinal arrangement of fibers in a plank of wood, as in, say, the 3¼-inch vertical-grain fir that might be used to patch the water damage in front of a kitchen sink, if slow-growth fir trees, harvested with abandon by West Coast loggers around the time when Sarah Siddons was performing, had not been supplanted by fast-growth firs, whose wood has the strength of balsa. It's possible that Barthes intends to conjure the agricultural sense of the word "grain"—with the voice being somehow akin to a grain of wheat—but the lumber allusion seems more promising, if equally baffling. I think, though I am not sure, that Barthes is trying to characterize that constellation of features that makes a person's voice instantly recognizable, the quality that allows my elderly mother to hear the two words "Hi Mom" through a long-distance phone line and know that it is me.[2]

In Barthes's essay "The Grain of the Voice," he is primarily concerned with making a subtle distinction between the singing voices of Dietrich Fischer-Dieskau and Charles Panzéra by means of Julia Kristeva's even subtler distinction between pheno-texts and geno-texts. Transposing Kristeva's terms, Barthes defines the pheno-song as "everything which, in the performance, is at the service of communication, of representation, of expression" (270), whereas the geno-song is not what language says, but "the voluptuous pleasure of its signifier-sounds," or "the *diction* of language" (271). "From the point of view of pheno-song, Fischer-Dieskau is certainly an irreproachable artist," Barthes writes, "yet nothing [in his performance] seduces, nothing persuades us to enjoyment" (271).

Jonathan Dunsby suggests that the terms Kristeva uses to describe language do not really help Barthes characterize what he means by "the grain of the voice." Dunsby writes, "His idea of 'grain' has become paradigmatic, floating free from its aetiology, possibly too even from its empirical justification."[3] Dunsby links Barthes's enthusiasm for Panzéra, from whom Barthes took voice lessons, to that singer's commitment to the "sheer physicality of vocal pedagogy" (120). Panzéra's 1945 *L'art de chanter* includes chapters on the breath, vocal apparatus, and bodily resonance. When Barthes complains that when he listens to Fischer-Dieskau sing, he never hears "the tongue, the glottis, the teeth, the sinuses, the nose," he does so as a Panzéra acolyte (271). Barthes, according to Dunsby, was searching "for embodiment, the audible presence of the singer; not just the song, but a physicality that he believed to be part of a largely lost world of Romantic intimacy between composer, singer, and audience" (123). Perhaps when Barthes, in his inimitable and somewhat inscrutable way, insists on the superiority of Panzéra's over Fischer-Dieskau's singing, he does so primarily because of his more intimate association with Panzéra. But even if the specific distinctions he uses to contrast the two singers do not hold up to musicological analysis, Barthes, the loyal student of a kinesthetically oriented voice teacher, directs our attention back to the singer's body and to the listener's bodily pleasure.

Before setting off on his Kristevan excursus, Barthes claims that what he has to say about the grain is only an "impossible accounting" for the enjoyment he experiences when he listens to singing (269). I was trying to carry out an impossible accounting for the enjoyment Joseph Severn and others experienced when they listened to Sarah Siddons perform. Severn claimed the tones of her "deep touching voice" were "like the finest music, for they thrilled the air with melodious tones."[4] This enjoyment, I speculated, was caused partly by the particular and specifically embodied qualities of Siddons's voice, the traits it exhibited as a result of being a product of Siddons's body and not that of another actor. Siddons's appeal, after all, could not be re-created from the texts of her speeches, which I'd read without having the slightest impulse to weep or swoon in the manner of her original audience members. And the same speeches had been voiced by many other actors, actors whose rendering of the lines inspired admiration, but not physical collapse.[5]

Siddons's disappointing debut at Drury Lane occurred decades before Severn heard her perform as Queen Katherine, and, apparently, before she'd achieved full control over her voice. The season did not end with her lackluster performance as Portia. She also processed silently across stage as the figure of Venus in Garrick's popular afterpiece *The Jubilee*, which was staged after *The Merchant of Venice* and also after many other plays during the 1775–76 season. *The Jubilee* was an excuse for reenacting a parade originally organized for a promotion of Shakespeare's birthplace at Stratford in 1769. Actors from the Drury Lane company, who, weather permitting, would have processed through the streets of Stratford in full Shakespearean costume, instead wound up marching, night after night, across the Drury Lane stage in a "gilt gingerbread" spectacle aimed at attracting latecomers to the theater; people who didn't get off work in time to watch the main play could go to see the showy afterpiece.[6]

The *Jubilee* procession served the same purpose as a sports highlight reel, allowing theater fans to recall scenes they knew so well that, in a pinch, the fans could have served as prompters. A chariot drawn by butterflies evoked a *Midsummer Night's Dream* tableau, and a ship in distress sailed downstage as part of a *Tempest* display. Audience members could recognize Malvolio because he walked across stage carrying a letter and wearing his stockings "cross Garter'd." An actress wearing night clothes and carrying a taper called to mind Lady Macbeth. Siddons was cast as Venus, one of the lesser figures that filled out the procession, and she was elbowed out of the way by rivalrous actresses. As she later recalled, "[The role] gained me the malicious appellation of *Garrick's Venus* and the ladies who so kindly bestowed it on me, so determinedly rushed before me in the last scene, that had he not broken through them all, and brought us forward with his own hand, my little Cupid and my self, whose appointed situations were in the very front of the stage, might have as well have been in the Island of Paphos at that moment."[7]

She was pushed off stage more definitively when she was not invited to return to Drury Lane for the following season. "Who may concieve [*sic*] the size of this cruel disappointment, this dreadful reverse of all my ambitious hopes," she wrote, describing the despondency into which she sank as a result of the "degradation" of being banished from Drury Lane (*Reminiscences*, 6–7). Thus began her seven-year-long sojourn in the theatrical desert. She spent the summer of 1776 performing in Birmingham and then alternated among Liverpool, Manchester, and York during the 1776–77 season. By the fall of 1778, she was performing at Bath and had established herself as the most popular and acclaimed actress in the provinces—seemingly by dint of brutal hard work. During her first season at Bath, at age twenty-four and pregnant with her third child, she took on thirty roles, and by the fall of 1779, she was playing the Shakespearean roles for which she would eventually become best known: Lady Macbeth, Queen Katherine, and Constance. During her engagement at Bath, she later recalled, "Tragedies which had been almost banished again resumed their proper interest" (*Reminiscences*, 7).

Something happened during Siddons's seven-year stint in the provinces that allowed her to consolidate her powers and to create a vocal brand that was reliably and recognizably Siddonian. Mladen Dolar describes the voice as something that points toward meaning, as an arrow "which raises the expectation of meaning."[8] He writes about intonation, the "particular tone of the voice, its particular melody and modulation, its cadence and inflection," as deciding the meaning of what is being spoken, and he calls the theater "the ultimate practical laboratory of endowing the same text with the shades of intonation and thereby bringing it to life" (21). Dolar points to some innate quality that leads us to anticipate meaning when we hear a voice—as we don't when listening, say, to the whir of a microfilm reader—and he suggests that the way in which an individual speaks words inevitably affects what those words communicate. During her seven years in the hinterlands Siddons cultivated a voice that made people hear familiar plays in a new way. Worn-out mainstays of an old theatrical repertoire suddenly became new again when they were transmitted by Siddons. There was something about the grain of her voice that penetrated her fans' consciousness and made them feel like they were seeing and hearing something totally new, even though they were seeing and hearing plays that had been performed for decades or even centuries, plays they hadn't thought they'd ever want to see again.

Siddons returned to Drury Lane in 1782, having been invited by Thomas Sheridan, now the theater's manager. Siddons recalled the lead-up to her Drury Lane performance in the role of Isabella as a struggle to calm her nervous anxiety over whether her voice would function properly. She wrote of the first rehearsal, "Who can imagine my terror? I fear'd to utter a sound above an audible whisper [for] some minutes, but by degrees enthusiasm cheated me into forgetfulness of my fears, and I unconsciously threw out my voice, which fail'd not to be heard in the remotest part of the House by a friend who kindly undertook to ascertain the happy circumstance" (*Reminiscences*, 9). But as her preparation continued, her concerns about her voice were never totally allayed. On the evening of the second rehearsal, she was "siezed [*sic*] with a nervous hoarseness" that made her wretched. She passed a sleepless night, but woke the next day, the day before her performance, to discover, upon speaking to her husband, that her voice was much clearer. On the morning of the scheduled performance, her voice "was most happily perfectly restored," but, taking no chances, she completed her dress "without uttering one word, though frequently sighing most profoundly" (*Reminiscences*, 10).

According to Siddons's version of events, the success of the performance depended primarily on the state of her voice, which may or may not have served her well in the actual event. When Sylas Neville saw her act the part eleven days later (Siddons played Isabella eight times during the three weeks after her first performance), he called her voice "pleasing," and noted that she excelled "in the pathetic."[9] Horace Walpole, who saw her a week after Neville, was equivocal on the subject of her voice, declaring it "clear and good," but also complaining that she did not "vary its modulations enough, nor ever approach enough to the familiar," although he went on to concede that "this may come when [she is] more habituated to the awe of the audience of the capital."[10] A reviewer for the *Morning Post* declared her "beyond all comparison . . . the first tragic actress now on the English stage," while also conceding that her portrayal of grief could tend to monotony and that her voice was sometimes raised inharmoniously.[11] Still, Boaden recalled "the *sobs*, the *shrieks*, among the tenderer part of her audiences" and how her performance led male audience members to give up their struggle to suppress tears (*Memoirs of Mrs. Siddons*, 1: 327).

That the *Morning Post* reviewer could confidently declare Siddons the premier tragic actress of the English stage even as he pinpointed small imperfections in her vocal presentation might be a result of the transitional nature of her performance style. As Robert Shaughnessy notes, her performances bridged a transition from neoclassicism to romanticism, "the first aspect becoming visible in a classically inspired, literally statuesque composition of posture, gesture, and costume which rendered her characters as legendary, iconic figures, the second element being found in the focused emotional intensity of her delivery."[12] Actors of Siddons's age "were all ponderous, measured, and 'tea-potish,'" recalls Fred Belton in his *Random Recollections of an Old Actor.* Siddons was one of the last practitioners of the teapot school of acting, so-called because of the actor's tendency to position herself with one hand thrust into the air and the other pressed to her bosom, in an approximation of a child's "I'm a little teapot" stance. Belton goes on to note that the exaggerated stance was evident in Mrs. Siddons's attitude "in that splendid picture, the Trial of Queen Catharine, in 'Henry the Eighth;' the pressure of the bosom by the one hand, and the unnatural elevation of the other, points evidently to it" (fig. 7).[13] The stylized stance was accompanied by a stylized voice that had, at the beginning of the adoption of this mode of acting, the kind of resonant trilling sound a teapot would emit if teapots could speak. Dion Boucicault, in *The Art of Acting* (1882), noted the shift in acting styles at the turn of the nineteenth century, and the concomitant voice alterations. He associated actors of the teapot school with the treble voice:—"They did it as if they played on the flute"—but noted that this style of voice was quickly followed by a period when "the tragedian played his part on the double bass *so*."[14] Siddons seems to have been performing on the cusp of a theater transition, and her voice may have vacillated between a more styl-ized older vocal tradition and a more naturalistic newer one. But even as certain audience members noticed the rifts in her vocal execution, they were still swept about by some compelling undercurrent in Sid-dons's voice, by what Barthes would call the grain.

At the end of "The Grain of the Voice" essay, Barthes seems to for-get that he set out to analyze his aesthetic preference for Panzéra over Fischer-Dieskau and starts finding grains everywhere. "The 'grain' is the body in the singing voice, in the writing hand, in the performing limb," he writes, leaving singers behind, and segueing without warning into a discussion of his favorite harpsichordist (276). "I hear without a doubt," he writes, "that Wanda Landowska's harpsichord comes from her inner body, and not from the minor digital knitting of so many harpsichordists" (277). I loved Barthes's strange image of lockstep in-strumentalists performing with Defargian precision.

One can describe the grain of a voice, Barthes decrees, but only through metaphors.[15] Of the voice of Gundula Janowitz, he writes, "That voice does indeed have a grain (at least to my ears); to describe this grain, I find images of a milkweed acidity, of a nacreous vibration, situated at the exquisite and dangerous limit of the *toneless*" ("Phan-toms," 184). Maria Callas's grain he calls "*tubular* . . . hollow, with a res-onance that is just a bit off-pitch" (184). Even though Barthes writes against the tyranny of the adjective in music criticism—"Are we doomed to the adjective? Are we faced with this dilemma: the predica-ble or the ineffable?" ("Grain of the Voice," 268)—his adjectives (milk-weed! nacreous!) stick with me, even as his postulations on signifier-sounds get shunted off to memory's remote storage unit, along with my eBay password and everything I once knew about the Krebs cycle. Writing about his effort to recover how David Garrick's voice sounded, Peter Holland evokes the kind of descriptive sentence that is a mainstay of romantic era memoirs and theater criticism: "To be told the follow-ing is not really to be told very much of use: 'Mr. Garrick's voice was clear, impressive, and affecting.'"[16] But perhaps the proliferation of such sentences bespeaks a world in which listeners felt no anxiety about describing their listening experiences adjectivally.

Barthes's grain-of-the-voice essay argues against the "predicative fa-tality," but it ends with Barthes detonating adjectives with the speed and accuracy of a nail gun (269). What James Wood writes about

Samuel Taylor Coleridge rings equally true of Barthes: "The great pathos, tension, and comedy of Coleridge's work is that he commits the sins he warns against—and commits them while in the act of warning against them."[17] Barthes and Coleridge had other things in common: a predilection for digression, a tendency to overintellectualize, a fondness for odd metaphors. Barthes never blamed a man from Porlock for causing him to write a lesser version of the perfect poem he was dreamily composing, but he, too, was constantly coming up with projects he would never finish, spinning his half-baked ideas into lovely souffles that collapsed if you made a loud noise. Would my study of Sarah Siddons's voice come to be described, like Coleridge's work, as a "perforated organum of allusion and enigmatic suggestion"?[18] I certainly hoped so, even though James Wood, I knew, didn't intend that description as a compliment.

Chapter Seven

Coleridge wrote a single poem about Sarah Siddons as part of a series of eleven "Sonnets on Eminent Characters," which he published in the *Morning Chronicle*. The poem's narrator describes the tales
told by a "Grandam," and in so doing makes reference to some of Siddons's famous roles. The grandmother conjures the witches in *Macbeth*
when she tells "of those hags, who at the witching time / Of murky
midnight ride the air sublime." She recalls a plot point of *The Tragedy of
Jane Shore* when she speaks "Of pretty babes, that lov'd each other dear,
/ Murder'd by cruel Uncle's mandate fell." As Coleridge's editor sum-
marizes the poem, "tales told to children affect them as Mrs Siddons,
acting similar tales, affects C[oleridge]."[1] My interest in the poem is
pretty much limited to the final couplet because that's where it becomes
clear that Coleridge is writing about Siddons's voice. There he writes of
"the shivering joys" her "tones impart," and professes her ability to
melt his "sad heart" (165).

When I teach Coleridge, I never assign the poem he wrote about
Siddons because it can't hold a candle to his best poems. We spend
nearly all of our time on "Christabel," a poem that circulated for over a
decade in manuscript and through oral transmission before it came out
in print.[2] I ask my students to memorize swaths of "Christabel," imagining a gala last-day-of-class choral reading that never quite pans out
because the students are nervous and speak their lines as if hurrying to
catch a bus. Occasionally a male student with a theatrical bent will get

into the spirit of Coleridge's metrical experiment, and emphasize each line's four accented syllables, punching the consonants as he speaks: "*Sir L*eoline, the *Bar*on *rich* / *Hath* a *tooth*less *mas*tiff *bitch*." But it's hard to replicate the bonhomie of a romantic era fireside recitation when you are sitting in a basement classroom and you're being graded. Certainly none of my students manages to match the emotional impact of Byron, who caused Shelley to run shrieking from the room when he spoke lines from "Christabel" at the Villa Diodati. Byron was reciting the part in which Geraldine disrobes and the narrator recoils:

> Behold! her bosom and half her side—
> Hideous, deformed, and pale of hue—
> O shield her! shield sweet Christabel!

Or perhaps he was reciting the revised version, with the line "Hideous, deformed, and pale of hue" replaced by the more enigmatic: "A Sight to dream of, not to tell!" (491). When Coleridge finally published the poem in 1816, the reviewer for the *Examiner* was so familiar with the manuscript version that he rebuked Coleridge for leaving out a line that he thought was necessary in order to make common sense of the poem; William Hazlitt called "Hideous, deformed, and pale of hue" "the keystone that makes up the arch" of the poem.[3] I usually don't show my students the less ambiguous version of the poem because it makes Geraldine a crone instead of a seductress. In the "Hideous" version, she's the cookie-cutter hag of a slasher film; in the "Sight to dream of" version, she can't be so easily placed. Usually students perk up for the poem's bedroom scene, with its whiff of lesbianism, and I can hold their attention longer if I dwell on Shelley's charged response to Byron's recitation. After he was calmed down by his doctor Polidori, who threw water in his face and gave him ether, Shelley confessed that he was looking at Mary Shelley and "suddenly thought of a woman he had heard of who had eyes instead of nipples, which, taking hold of his mind, horrified him."[4] Ken Russell's film *Gothic* immortalized the nipple moment, materializing Shelley's scary thought by having Claire Clairmont's breasts blink open and stare at Shelley. The film doesn't manage to convey, however, that *listening* to Byron speak the lines of Coleridge's poem made Shelley recall *hearing* about a woman with eyes for nipples. The disturbing all-seeing breasts were the product of two separate aural encounters.

It's easy to overlook how immersed romantic poets were in the way poetry sounded, but thinking about romantic poetry as it was conveyed out loud makes it easier to understand why the romantic poets were ardent theatergoers, and why several of them were Siddons devotees. Byron's recitation of part of Coleridge's poem was one link in a long line of oral transmission. Coleridge recited the poem for the benefit of William and Dorothy Wordsworth in 1800. In 1802, John Stoddart recited the poem for Sir Walter Scott. Scott recited the poem for Byron, who recalled, "All took a hold on my imagination which I never shall wish to shake off."[5] And Shelley, months after Byron's recitation made him flee a room, gave a "quiet memorial reading" of Coleridge's poem to Mary before going to bed.[6] For years, the poem we know as "Christabel" was a performance piece—and whether it was terrifying or soothing depended on who spoke the lines.

Coleridge's poem on Siddons, in contrast, never inspired anyone to recite its lines. The poem wobbles a bit in places—Coleridge jettisoned a necessary "to" in order to preserve the fourth line's ten-syllable pentameter, and thus a child in the opening quatrain "Listens strange tales of fearful dark decrees." The confusing syntax is matched by a confusing provenance. The essayist Charles Lamb refers to the poem as his own in a letter seeking Coleridge's improvements. The poem may have been written by both men, Coleridge's editor suggests, "conjointly, in a way which left neither of them clear about his respective claims" (Coleridge, 164). Lamb's involvement makes the sonnet's final couplet

Ev'n such the shiv'ring joys thy tones impart,
Ev'n so thou, SIDDONS! meltest my sad heart! (165)

more interesting, given Lamb's notorious ambivalence about the voice's impact; he suggested Shakespeare's plays were better read than performed. "*Speaking*, whether it be in soliloquy or dialogue, is only a medium," he wrote, "and often a highly artificial one, for putting the reader or spectator into possession of that knowledge of the inner structure and workings of mind in a character."[7]

Lamb's reference to the voice as a medium calls to mind the media triangle that scholars of communication studies use to explain the workings of media. Such scholars view media as having three interrelated dimensions—content, transmitter, and audience.[8] The triangle formulation emphasizes that all three components of media are part of an interlocking system, and that meaning gets communicated through the interaction of the three dimensions that make up the triangle's sides. A good teacher of the media triangle concept will help students see how content, transmitter, and audience are each individually composed of a number of factors and interactions. If we think about Siddons's performances in the framework provided by this formulation, we might position the play script as content, Siddons's fans as audience, and her voice as transmitter. We would keep in mind that there are many other features influencing transmission in general (staging, costumes, lighting), and voice in particular (vocal hygiene, acoustics, ambient noise), and also that the other legs of the triangle (content, audience) could each also be subdivided into many different factors, all of which would impinge on how the voice is received. The media triangle, that is, provides another means of emphasizing the one-off nature of performance.

But it can also help us understand paradigm-shifting moments in media history. The most radically minimalist definitions of media, such as those of Marshall McLuhan and Friedrich Kittler, John Peters notes, require only the second term of the triad—a transmitter—"leaving messages and people as add-ons" (266). For Marshall McLuhan, famously, the medium (transmitter) is the message (content), since the "message" of any medium of technology is "the change of scale or pace or pattern that it introduces into human affairs," the way it shapes and controls the forms of human association and action.[9] We might ask, following McLuhan's paradigm, whether Siddons's voice as transmitter overwhelmed the content it conveyed. If you think of Siddons's voice as a new and startling kind of transmitter, listening to it in its original context must have seemed like hearing Alexander Graham Bell's first words over a telephone wire or Thomas Edison's earliest recordings of the human voice—the words were not as important as the astonishing new way in which they were being transmitted. Perhaps Siddons became the phenomenon that she was because her voice had the impact of a new media. Her voice wasn't saying anything new—her audience was more than familiar with the repertoire of plays from which she spoke lines. But she spoke them in such a distinctive new manner that her voice had the same kind of impact as an innovation in sound-producing technology. When Maria Edgeworth heard Siddons read portions of *Henry VIII* she was moved to comment, "I felt that I had never before fully understood or sufficiently admired Shakespeare, or known the full powers of the human voice and the English language" (Campbell, *Life of Mrs. Siddons*, 2: 351). Listening to Siddons was like switching from monophonic to stereophonic sound, like replacing a television's rabbit ears with a rooftop antenna.

But even if Siddons caused transmission to trump content and audience, her voice's reception was still part of a larger confluence of factors (theater size, audience tastes) that were morphing over her long career and also after her death, when the media triangle shifted again. Those fans who had heard Siddons perform now heard her voice through the transmissions of memory. And today, those who seek to know how Siddons sounded must rely on impressions of her voice that were written down soon after she performed, as well as recollections of her voice that were committed to paper years after the fact. An original Siddons media triangle might feature the script of *Macbeth* (content), Siddons's voice (transmitter), and the fans who filled Drury Lane or Covent Garden theater (audience). But for present-day would-be listeners, the Siddons media triangle consists of Siddons's voice (content), written memoirs of people who heard her perform (transmitter), and theater historians (audience).

Lamb's comment on the voice as a medium appears in his essay "On the Tragedies of Shakspeare, Considered with Reference to their Fitness for Stage Representation," and Lamb's considered opinion is that most of Shakespeare's plays are not suited for stage representation. *King Lear* serves as one example. "The Lear of Shakespeare cannot be acted," Lamb insists. "To see an old man tottering about the stage with a walking-stick, turned out of doors by his daughters in a rainy night," he writes, "has nothing in it but what is painful and disgusting" (107). Much of Lamb's aversion to seeing Shakespeare performed can be traced to a tradition of antitheatricalism that far predates the romantic period.[10] When Lamb shudders at coming across the "affected attitude" of the figure of actor David Garrick in Westminster Abbey, or when he objects that Garrick, who shone "in every drawling tragedy that his wretched day produced," should dwell in the mind as "an inseparable concomitant with Shakespeare," Lamb reveals his general aversion to the theater as a place of tawdry plays and even tawdrier offstage behavior (97, 104)

Lamb celebrates "the delightful sensation of freshness" with which

we turn to those Shakespeare plays "which have escaped being performed," and he despairs at how "the very custom of hearing any thing
spouted, withers and blows upon a fine passage" (99). Lamb seems to
conjure here the spouting clubs that gave amateur actors a venue for
trying out their impersonations of, say, Garrick playing Richard III,
and he bemoans the fate of those speeches "which are current in the
mouths of schoolboys" from their being found in *Enfield's Speaker* and
other popular recitation manuals of the day.[11] "I confess myself utterly
unable to appreciate that celebrated soliloquy in Hamlet," he writes, "it
has been so handled and pawed about by declamatory boys and men,
and torn so inhumanly from its living place and principle of continuity
in the play, till it is become to me a perfect dead member" (99).

Coleridge, who was capable of imagining an erotic world in which a
woman tells a story of being kidnapped by five warriors in order to in-
sinuate herself into another woman's bedroom, was untroubled by his
poem circulating freely, passing from the lips of Stoddart into the ears
of Scott, from the mouth of Byron into the suggestible mind of Shelley.
He seems to have viewed the voice as an enhancer of his lines. Even
though, in the better, more enigmatic version of "Christabel," his narrator calls Geraldine's bosom "a sight to dream of, not to tell!", the rest
of the poem emphasizes the uncanniness of spoken communication.
Geraldine's voice is "faint and sweet" when Christabel first discovers
her in the woods beyond her father's castle gate, but when Christabel
conjures the protective spirit of her dead mother, Geraldine responds
with first an "altered" and then a "hollow" voice, which she uses to rasp,
"Off, woman, off! this hour is mine— / Though thou her guardian
spirit be, / Off, woman, off! 'tis given to me." Coleridge's poem, to be
sure, dramatizes failures of communication—the dense Sir Leoline
misinterprets a dream that couldn't be any more transparent in its mir-
roring of his daughter's plight—but it also emphasizes the disturbing
allure of human and even subhuman vocalizations. When Geraldine's
eyes each "shrunk up to a serpent's eye," and Christabel responds by
shuddering aloud with a hissing sound, we are enthralled by this odd
call and response.

Lamb objected, in particular, to the theatergoers' tendency to identify the actor with the character whom he represents. "It is difficult for
a frequent play-goer to disembarrass the idea of Hamlet from the person and voice of Mr. K," he writes. "We speak of Lady Macbeth, while

we are in reality thinking of Mrs. S." (98). Byron too had Siddons's voice imprinted on his memory. He claimed that when he read Lady Macbeth's part, he had Siddons before him, and "imagination even supplie[d] her voice, whose tones were superhuman, and power over the heart supernatural."[12] Siddons's striking vocal performances, both Lamb's comments and Coleridge's "Christabel" indirectly confirm, inevitably enhanced her eroticism and focused attention on her sexuality, attention that she tried to neutralize by cultivating a private persona of perfect rectitude.

Siddons was so concerned about maintaining her reputation for propriety that she refused to meet Mary Robinson (the actress turned royal mistress turned literary figure), worried lest the association "however laudable or innocent . . . draw down the malice and reproach of those prudent people who never do ill."[13] Siddons was so intent on burnishing her public persona as a blameless matron that she once trotted her three children out on stage and recited a lengthy rhymed address highlighting her maternal devotion. "These are the moles that bear me from your side / Where I was rooted—where I could have died," she announced, presenting the children as the reason why she needed to leave Bath for London (Campbell, *Life of Mrs. Siddons*, 1: 91). Her maternal solicitude was stagy—the playbill for that evening announced that she would reveal "Three Reasons" why she was leaving Bath at the end of the performance, so a cynical observer would have to view the children's appearance as a publicity stunt.[14] Siddons deployed her children in order to emphasize her maternal solicitude so that she'd be at less risk of being besmirched by the powerful eroticism of her stage performances.

Lamb's phobic reaction to the erotics of the voice goes a long way toward explaining why he and his sister transformed Shakespeare's plays into tales that could be read by children, and, most particularly, by girls, who, unlike their brothers, would not have early access to Shakespeare's works. "Because boys are generally permitted the use of their fathers' libraries at a much earlier age than girls are," Lamb writes in the preface to *Tales from Shakespeare*, "they frequently hav[e] the best scenes of Shakespear by heart, before their sisters are permitted to look into this manly book."[15] Lamb calls on boys to kindly assist their sisters by explaining "such parts as are hardest for them to understand," and by reading passages that are "proper for a young sister's ear" (2).

Having the best scenes of Shakespeare by heart, those protective brothers might have noted the way Lamb laundered some of Lady Macbeth's most disturbing lines so that they were less traumatizing for the nursery set. Into the mouth of Lady Macbeth, Shakespeare put these lines:

> I have given suck, and know
> How tender 'tis to love the babe that milks me;
> I would, while it was smiling in my face,
> Have plucked my nipple from his boneless gums
> And dashed the brains out, had I so sworn
> As you have done to this.[16]

Out of the mouth of Lady Macbeth, Lamb whisked these lines and gave them, instead, to a third-person narrator who flatly reports that Lady Macbeth "declared that she had given suck, and knew how tender it was to love the babe that milked her, but she would, while it was smiling in her face, have plucked it from her breast, and dashed its brains out, if she had so sworn to do it, as he had sworn to perform that murder" (94). Lady Macbeth's nipple and her baby's boneless gums get airbrushed out of the picture. The close-up details of lactation, for Lamb, are more disturbing than infanticide.

Charles and Mary Lamb published *Tales from Shakespeare* in 1807. Their flat rendition of Lady Macbeth's famous speeches must surely be haunted by the auditory ghost of Siddons's ineluctable performance in that role. By placing Siddons in a media triangle framework, we can imagine her voice as a new kind of transmitter. The impression it made on her listeners, the way it became indelibly inscribed on the memories of Byron and Lamb, supports this characterization. If we rotate the triangle, as I'd like to do now, in order to think about Siddons's voice as a form of content that was being transmitted via changing theater acoustics, our attention must turn to the way in which Siddons's voice got mutated by the resonating cavities of particular theaters.

Chapter Eight

Siddons's performing career spanned four decades during which time London theaters were being steadily enlarged, sometimes as a result of their tendency to burst into flame. The Covent Garden theater, which in 1792 housed 1,897 theater patrons, succumbed to fire in 1808; after it was redesigned and reopened, it could accommodate 3,000 audience members. The Drury Lane theater in which Siddons made her London debut could hold 2,000 theatergoers; it was replaced in 1794 by a theater that could hold 3,611 people. This cavernous space, designed by Henry Holland, caught on fire in 1809 and was supplanted in 1811 by a new theater designed by Benjamin Wyatt. Wyatt's theater brought about a small retrenchment in audience capacity—it could hold 3,060 people, 551 fewer than Holland's theater could accommodate, but, still, it was a huge venue, a third again the size of the theater that had stood in its place throughout most of the eighteenth century.

We stand at a moment in history when "theaters" have shrunk and listening experiences have been refined and personalized. David Denby, describing the novel experience of watching *Pirates of the Caribbean* on an iPod screen, despairs of the "pipsqueak" display that makes Johnny Depp and Orlando Bloom duel "like two angry mosquitoes in a jar." "In a theatre, you *submit* to a screen," Denby writes, "not struggle to get cozy with it." But he also describes the enhanced audio experience that comes from wearing headphones rather than from, say, listening in company with a fellow cineaste who may be slowly unwrapping a throat lozenge, creating a sonic equivalent of drip torture. As Denby watches miniaturized pirates duel on his iPod screen, he reports that his ears, "fed by headphones, were filled with such details as the chafing of hawsers and feet stomping on straw."[1] As Jonathan Sterne has noted, at the core of all advancements in sound recording technology "is the isolation, separation, and transformation of the senses themselves" (50). The movie theater has been rendered small enough so that anyone can carry a film screen in his pocket, and the film's audio component has been tailored to suit the isolated listener. This personalization of listening experience follows logically from the advent of sound recording technology, which created higher expectations for sound fidelity, the rise of the fussy audiophile, and the impetus for endless, tedious debates over vinyl versus digital recording.

Siddons, by contrast, performed at a moment when it was growing increasingly difficult to hear actors, since they were performing in larger houses that placed new demands on actors' voices, and that provided listeners with new forms of distraction. Walking into the newly enlarged Drury Lane theater of 1794 was like walking into a giant wedding cake that had been turned inside out so that all the furbelows and rosette garlands were on the interior walls. When Siddons reprised the role of Isabella at Drury Lane in 1796, she sent her voice up into a cylinder with tiers of ornate balconies hanging over her head, and she had difficulty projecting in what she called "a wilderness of a place."[2]

How big a theater wilderness does it take to contain 3,600 people? I wondered casually, and then more intently, as I realized that I could no more estimate the number of audience members in a large theater than I could guess the number of jelly beans in a large jar. An hour later, having Googled the seating charts of some of the world's greatest theaters, and having interrogated the receptionists at a few regional theaters, and having irritated the secretaries at two local learning establishments, I had the data I needed to compare the vast wilderness of the Drury Lane theater circa 1796 to the modest suburbs of some competing venues.

Carnegie Hall—Isaac Stern Auditorium (New York)	2,804 seats
La Scala (Milan)	2,800 seats
Hancher Auditorium (University of Iowa, Iowa City—before the flood)	2,553 seats
Royal Opera House (London)	2,268 seats

Lost Colony outdoor amphitheatre (Roanoke Island)   1,396 seats

Iowa City High School auditorium (Iowa City)   750 seats

Siddons wasn't the only one who was disturbed by the number of human beings who could be stacked on top of each other in London theaters. Sir Walter Scott complained that the magnitude of theaters had "occasioned them to be destined to company so scandalous, that persons not very nice in their taste of society, must yet exclaim against the abuse as a national nuisance." He was especially disturbed by "a certain description of female," who in theaters of moderate size "would feel themselves compelled to wear a mask at least of decency," but who in larger theaters felt no compunction to conceal "the open display of [their] disgusting improprieties."[3] But he also regretted how large-scale theaters altered the nature of performance. "The persons of the performers are, in these huge circles, so much diminished, that nothing short of the mask and buskin could render them distinctly visible to the audience," he complained, going on to lament the show and machinery that had come to usurp the place of tragic poetry since "the author is compelled to address himself to the eyes, not to the understanding or feelings of the spectators" (463). Even though George Colman, quoting Macbeth, described the much smaller Haymarket theater as "cabined, cribbed, and confined," he still preferred this more intimate venue to the Drury Lane and Covent Garden theaters. "However the audience in this little theatre might be cramped for room and accommodation," he wrote, "they certainly could hear and see the performers upon its stage better than upon those covered Salisbury Plains which now characterize the two grand winter houses."[4]

   The playwright Joanna Baillie believed that larger theaters were replacing acting with pantomime.[5] She did not fault audience members for enjoying an "inferior species of entertainment" made possible by big theaters—that is, spectacular entertainments—especially since the nuances of more serious drama were increasingly difficult to hear. But she mourned the demise of well-spoken soliloquy. "What actor in his senses will then think of giving to the solitary musing of a perturbed mind that muttered, imperfect articulation which grows by degrees into words; that heavy, suppressed voice as of one speaking through sleep; that rapid burst of sounds which often succeeds the slow languid tones of distress; those sudden, untuned exclamations which, as if frightened at their own discord, are struck again into silence as sudden and abrupt, with all the corresponding variety of countenance that belongs to it?" (xx–xxi). No, she countered, an actor in the new, overly large theaters would, instead, plant himself in the middle of the stage and tell all the secrets of his heart "in an audible uniform voice" (xxi). Hazlitt shared Baillie's concern about the diminution of the voice. "We hear the din and bray of the orchestra," he wrote, "not the honeyed words of the poet; and still we wonder that operas and melo-drames flourish, and that the legitimate stage and good old English Comedy languishes."[6]

Siddons performed at a moment when architects were beginning to figure out how far the voice carried in different acoustic settings, and to design theaters so that they would transport sound effectively. In his 1790 *Treatise on Theatres*, George Saunders explained that, in designing a theater, the first question that naturally arises is, "In what form does the voice expand?"[7] Saunders carried out a series of experiments in which he traced circles of varying diameter around a speaker and then noted at which point on the circle a listener would be able to hear the speaker best (if at all). He believed that voices behaved differently than other fixed sounds, and became convinced of the "delicate nature of the voice, and of the trifling circumstances that will check it in its progress" (8). "The lightness of air and gentle impulsions occasioned by the voice, will account for its not getting readily around any obstacle," Saunders continued, going on to say, "The time necessary for its arrival gives opportunity for its being destroyed."[8]

It's possible to see Siddons's London career as the struggle of a voice to make itself heard in difficult circumstances, to regard her voice as the plucky victim of increasingly cavernous theaters. Siddons began her career acting in provincial barns and make-do spaces of mostly modest size, but she performed on the London stage during a period when the actor was being placed in less and less intimate contact with audience members. David Garrick, the actor-manager who first brought Siddons to London, ended the tradition of audience members lounging about on stage. He also championed the development of increasingly elaborate lighting effects, such as the installation of lights in a border position behind the proscenium, a change that pushed actors upstage into the scenery area.[9] Theatrical extravaganza became de rigeur: battle scenes with live horses, light shows that simulated waterfalls.

Given that I can't hear Siddons at all, it may seem ridiculous that I regret particularly not being able to hear her in a particular theater. But Siddons surely sounded different in each of the theaters in which she performed, and I'd most like to hear how her voice bounced off, or was absorbed by, the tiers of seating in one of the two main London theaters where she spent most of her career. The aural architecture of a particular setting is "the composite of numerous surfaces, objects, and geometries in a complicated environment," and no interior was more complicated than the interior of Drury Lane.[10] For me to understand what caused audience members to swoon when Siddons performed, it wouldn't be enough to teleport her voice into my current soundscape, where it would mingle with the burble of a coffee maker downstairs, and the intermittent chatter of a keyboard in another room. I would need to hear her voice as it competed with the rustle of audience members in varying states of attention.

You can get a fine sense of the scale of the Drury Lane theater by looking at Edward Dayes's 1795 drawing of the interior, with its depiction of three tiny actors acting before five tiers of audience members in varying states of distraction (fig. 10). Dayes angled his portrait so that we'd look from the perspective of a spectator sitting somewhere near the back of the bench seats in the pit, and we can see the row of orchestra musicians lined up with their backs to the stage, and the decorative grill separating the musicians from the first row of spectators. In many ways the theater—with its ornate domed ceiling, its scalloped blue drapery, its clusters of candlelight—seems perfectly configured to distract attention away from the main stage. The stack of lattice-framed boxes makes the stage seem like it has been multiplied into a film strip. One's eye wanders up and down the frames while the actors labor off to the side like an afterthought.

The sound historian Emily Thompson, describing a photograph of the New York Life Insurance Building, which was especially designed to protect workers from ambient noise, acknowledges the difficulty of using visual images to elicit the lost reverberations of the past. In the photograph one can almost see the acoustically treated ceilings installed to absorb the din of clattering dishes, Thompson points out, but it's impossible to see the sound itself: "Such everyday sounds are virtually always lost to the historian."[11] Looking at Dayes's portrait of Drury Lane, we can't see the noise caused by an irate audience member who,

Fig. 10. Edward Dayes, Drury Lane interior (1795), Courtesy of the Huntington Library, Art Collections, and Botanical Gardens, San Marino, California.

in waving his cane, mirrors the gestures of the fencers on stage. The kerfuffle he causes rivets the attention of the entire back half of the pit, while nearby, in the boxes, audience members turn their heads to catch wisps of private conversation.

For actors, maintaining acoustic control of the theater was fraught with peril since theater attendees felt no obligation to sit in respectful silence. Edmund Kean was so infuriated by the sounds of nut cracking emanating from the gallery of a theater in which he was performing that he gave instructions to his followers to buy up every nut in town. Spurred by the sudden increase in nut demand, local fruiterers increased their stocks. The actor Squire Bancroft recalls, "Crack!—crack!—crack! was the running fire throughout the succeeding performances, and the rest of Kean's engagement was fulfilled in torment."[12] But just as often, audience noise was purposeful rather than inadvertent. Anticipating the popularity of sing-along *Sound of Music* screenings, romantic era audiences enjoyed screaming in tandem with Siddons.[13] On one occasion, after a "paragraphical assassin" cast aspersions on Siddons in the press, claiming she was avaricious and uncharitable, a theater audience loudly voiced disapproval of the actress. When the curtain went up on Siddons performing as Mrs. Beverley in *The Gamester*, she "was saluted with violent hissing, and a cry of *off! off!* intermixed with applause." Siddons tried to speak but could not make herself heard; her brother John Kemble escorted her off stage. An hour passed before the audience tumult was silenced sufficiently for Siddons to be able to retake the stage, declare her innocence, and carry on as Mrs. Beverley. But her enemy in the press continued to spread stories of her parsimony, whispering with great joy, "*You see what a noise I've made!*"[14]

The vulnerability of the voice was a subject of more quotidian and material concern for theatergoers straining to hear actors who had to throw their voices greater distances to the detriment of emotional nuance. Just as silent movie stars with unpleasant speaking voices saw their careers shrink with the advent of sound in film, so did actors known for subtle enunciation rather than grand pronouncements suffer from the enlargement of theaters. Of Siddons's contemporary John Henderson, an actor praised for his ability to play "all the mellow varieties of ingenious or humorous or designing conversation," Boaden lamented, "I fear we have less chance than ever of such perfection—the voice in large theatres is taken out of the scale for these delicate inflexions of tone" (*Memoirs of Mrs. Siddons*, 2: 30). Henderson's undertones, according to Boaden, could not be heard at any distance. Boaden writes, "Had I never seen him but at Drury Lane, I should not have conceived him to be the great actor that he really was" (1: 170). Projecting the voice in such a theater required great feats of strength, and audiences sympathized with these efforts. Hazlitt recalled watching Edmund Kean perform in *Richard III* when his voice had not entirely recovered its "tone and strength" from the night before. When a Mr. Rae came forward to announce the play for Monday, "cries of 'No, no,' from every part of the house, testified the sense entertained by the audience, of the impropriety of requiring the repetition of this extraordinary effort, till every physical advantage had been completely removed."[15]

Audience, theater architects, actors—all viewed actors' voices as shrinking violets venturing out into the unforgiving soundscape of the theater, where they could be trampled or ignored. We might regard the voices we are used to hearing in modern theaters and auditoriums as hardier entities because their passage has been cleared and smoothed by revolutions in theater design. Theaters and auditoriums are now typically constructed in a fan shape so that the voice can travel unimpeded from the performer's mouth to the listener's ear. And the kind of reverberation that once gave theaters like Drury Lane distinct acoustic signatures has been reconceived as noise and erased by acoustic materials aimed at stopping sounds from careening around a room and reinforcing a voice with echoey ghost versions of itself.[16]

In one plausible representation of Siddons's career, all indicators point to her voice being displaced by a flurry of special effects and by overwhelmingly large theaters that dwarfed actors and made their voices inaudible or expendable. "The play and the players . . . dwindle into insignificance," wrote Hazlitt, "and are lost in the blaze of a huge chandelier or the grin of a baboon."[17] It's a romantic era version of *The Phantom of the Opera*, with everyone waiting to see the chandelier plummet, except in Hazlitt's account they are waiting to see "a castle set on fire by Mr. Farley."[18] According to one narrative of events, the Licensing Act of 1737, with its tightening of government control over "spoken drama," fueled the proliferation of nonspoken drama and the rise of spectacle. But the Licensing Act also ensured the ongoing viability of creaky but pre-vetted theatrical vehicles that didn't have to meet the approval of the Lord Chamberlain, plays that Siddons brought newly to life. "The audience of the metropolis had been for many years deprived, by the want of skilful tragedians," Elizabeth Inchbald writes in her introduction to *Isabella*, going on to say that "[Siddons] enchanted all the town by her 'well painted passion,' and established in the dramatic world, the long lost prerogative of sighs and tears."[19] "The Theatre overflowed every night she appeared," wrote the author of *The Secret History of the Green Rooms*, "and Melpomene, who had been pushed behind the curtain by the satire of SHERIDAN'S *Critic*, resumed her former consequence and station."[20] In the acoustic chaos of Drury Lane or Covent Garden, while performing in a repertoire of down-at-the-heels tragedies that had been shoved aside by showier fare, Siddons somehow managed to cause people to prick up their ears.

Chapter Nine

Not long after I started thinking about Siddons's voice, I read an article by J. Paul Hunter that came to hover over my endeavors like the little cloud that is stalled over Blake's piper in the introduction to *Songs of Innocence*. In the article, Hunter talks about aesthetic forms that lose their intended audience as standards of taste radically change. His case in point: the heroic couplet, once the lingua franca of the Enlightenment, and now a form tainted by its association with imperialist ideology. Hunter catalogs the form's attributes: "The couplet is smug, reductive, precise, rationalized, disciplined, rigid, calculatedly and ruthlessly balanced, and constructed for quick, striking and simplistic short-term impact."[1] But he goes on to suggest that "in historical texts and modes"—even discredited ones, perhaps *especially* discredited ones (well, he doesn't say that, but I do)—"there are often Sleeping Beauties that it would be lovely to see awakened again" (18). Many of the plays in which Siddons performed contain Sleeping Beauties, but so do other literary works of the period. Romantic poetry can be just as alienating as the heroic couplet; students often fail to perceive its charms, and occasionally even resort to calling Shelley a whiner or Wordsworth a bore.

Ever since I'd become preoccupied with Siddons's voice, I'd been reading romantic poems as the inscriptions of a people who didn't know the phonograph would soon arrive, but who, nevertheless, were preoccupied with the problem of how to fix the voice in time. I flipped through the pages of my graduate student edition of Wordsworth, the book's bland green cover opening to reveal inky nests of student-annotated poems. My slavish miniature transcriptions of professors' comments shed no light on my current obsession—no pencil marks sullied the margins of Wordsworth's Preface to the 1815 *Poems*, in which he discusses lines about the song of a stock dove ("His voice was *buried* among trees, / Yet to be come at by the breeze").[2] No sonorous lecturer from my educational past had caused me to notice that Wordsworth characterizes the dove's vocalization as "not partaking of the shrill and the piercing, and therefore more easily deadened by the intervening shade," but also as "a note so peculiar, and withal so pleasing, that the breeze, gifted with that love of the sound which the Poet feels, penetrates the shade in which it is entombed, and conveys it to the ear of the listener."[3] I alone, while passing a quiet office hour, my doorway shadowed by students queuing for the modernist down the hall, marveled at Wordsworth's attention to the stock dove's song. My discovery of his observations in the same pages where I'd once written "loaded with perceptual acts" and "first person acts of cognitive aggression" next to the opening lines of "Tintern Abbey" gave my preoccupation with Siddons's voice an added solidity—here was more evidence that the romantic poets were fascinated with voices.

Even though Siddons is best remembered for her Lady Macbeth performance, which she inaugurated at Drury Lane in 1785, in her own day she was equally, if not more, famous for a quintet of less enduring roles: Isabella in Thomas Southerne's *Isabella; or, The Fatal Marriage*, the title character in Nicholas Rowe's *The Tragedy of Jane Shore*, Euphrasia in Arthur Murphy's *The Grecian Daughter*, Belvidera in Thomas Otway's *Venice Preserved*, and Zara in William Congreve's *The Mourning Bride*. Siddons put these plays into rotation during the 1782–83 Drury Lane season, which she began with her acclaimed 10 October Isabella performance, before going on to play Euphrasia on 30 October, Jane Shore on 8 November, Belvidera on 14 December, and Zara on 18 March. When the season was over, she reprised her Isabella, Belvidera, Euphrasia, and Jane Shore performances during the Dublin summer season, and then played Isabella again in London at the beginning of the 1783–84 season.

In playing Belvidera or Isabella or Jane Shore or Zara or Euphrasia, Siddons made the most of her vocal strength, communicating large emotions in an operatic style. If Siddons were an *American Idol* contestant, you might say she seized every melismatic opportunity to take a note and corkscrew up and down the scale in the manner of Mariah Carey. Hazlitt claimed, "It was in bursts of indignation, or grief, in sudden exclamations, in apostrophes and inarticulate sounds, that she raised the soul of passion to its height, or sunk it in despair."[4] Opera critics use the phrase "ecstatic listening" to describe how opera audiences anticipate opera high points, those moments when the singer pushes her voice to the limits of its capacity.[5] But theater audiences, too, often listen ecstatically for an actor to put a unique topspin on a line of text and loft it into the rafters. Dame Edith Evans's famous line-reading of the phrase "A handbag?" in *The Importance of Being Earnest*— she registered Lady Bracknell's outrage by means of a full-octave portamento—became a sonic highlight of the play that Evans's successors ignored at their peril. Judi Dench, who played the role in 1982, recalled, "After the line, people in the audience would say 'ohh' disappointedly and shuffle in their seats making it pretty obvious that they felt it had hardly been worth coming."[6]

Siddons's most celebrated roles all seemed to contain sonic highlights that were anticipated with pleasure. When Siddons, playing Euphrasia in *The Grecian Daughter,* had the opportunity in the first act to "throw out some of its most striking tones," she made the audience tremble when, "in a voice that never broke nor faltered in its climax, she thus to earth and Heaven denounced the tyrant" (Boaden, *Memoirs of Mrs. Siddons,* 1: 312–13). When she played Jane Shore during the 1790–91 Drury Lane season (during which she also reprised her Isabella, Euphrasia, and Zara performances), a German visitor to London was thrilled by the moment in the play when Jane approaches the door of a friend whose lover she has won away: "I shall never forget her in this situation, never forget the tone of her voice in answer to the servant, never the timidity, the anguish of her expression and movements."[7]

A volume gathering observations on Siddons performing her famous (but now little known) characters, published in 1784 "by a Lady," draws our attention to the way her dramatic realizations were premised on particular vocal effects. The lady notes that Siddons did not really "feel herself" Belvidera until the third speech, "when all that melting tenderness of voice" first struck the listener's ear, and she praises how Siddons's utterance of a single "Oh!" gave the full expression of her feelings.[8] Describing Siddons's performance as Isabella, especially the moment when Siddons swore her innocence and gave her dying laugh, the lady writes, "I must break off—Upon the whole, as there is but one feeling excited in this play, and that of such an overbearing nature, in the end annihilating all tender sensations, it unavoidably must have the same effect upon our sentiments, when we wish to describe them" (22–23). She claims that the feeling evoked by the memory of Siddons's vocalizations is so intense that she can't bear to go on writing her description of them, but write on she does, cataloging the highlights of Siddons's melodramatic roles.

It's possible to condense Siddons's repertoire to a list of ecstatic listening opportunities:

1. Belvidera's scream in *Venice Preserved*

2. Isabella's scream in Southerne's *Isabella; or, The Fatal Marriage*

3. Jane Shore's scream in *The Tragedy of Jane Shore*

4. Lady Randolph's expected scream in John Home's *Douglas*, which Siddons didn't supply, thereby establishing her extreme originality

The first of these most thrilling vocalizations came near the end of the fifth act of *Venice Preserved*. An engraving of a Thomas Stothard portrait of Siddons as Belvidera takes two lines from the final act as its caption: "The winds; hark how they whistle; / and the rain beats: Oh! how the weather shrinks me!" (fig. 11). In the portrait, Siddons, looking distressed and wearing a remarkably intricate hairdo for an actress playing a mad scene, clasps her hands to her right shoulder.[9] The caption's lines are spoken by Belvidera just before Jaffeir's ghost rises in what is almost certainly the scream scene. Belvidera must have screamed when Jaffeir's ghost arose, or, perhaps, she screamed a few lines afterward when Jaffeir's ghost "sinks." It's also possible that Belvidera screamed a beat later when the ghosts of both Jaffeir and his fellow conspirator Pierre rise "both bloody," or that she screamed before dying. The text of the University of Nebraska edition of *Venice Preserved* doesn't even mention the scream, but you can't *read* a scream in any event, except in comic books (A-A-A-A-A-A-H-H-H-H!!!). What we're left with, instead, is the unhelpful comment of the anonymous author of *Observations on Mrs. Siddons*. "Who shall give an idea of her shriek at the account of Jaffier's death," she asks, without bothering to answer her own question (8).

Fig. 11. James Heath after Thomas Stothard, *Mrs. Siddons as Belvidera in "Venice Preserved," Act V, Scene 5* (1783). This item is reproduced by permission of The Huntington Library, San Marino, California.

Siddons's audiences clearly went to these performances knowing exactly what they would be experiencing and looking forward to experiencing the extreme emotions that Siddons reliably elicited.[10] In a poetic tribute to Siddons, part of a 1788 volume of transcribed poems dedicated to Siddons, R. Bransby Cooper wrote, "She speaks—our passive breasts obedient move / We pity, scorn, detest, admire, or Love."[11] It is tempting to view Siddons's audience members as naively appreciative of an acting style that we would find overwrought. But romantic era theater enthusiasts could be swept away by the power of her acting, even while conscious of its stylized or excessive quality. It is not necessarily that they saw naturalness where we would see hyperbolic acting. Thomas Rowlandson's caricature of Siddons rehearsing in the green room (see fig. 5), published at the height of Siddons mania, makes manifest the exaggerated nature of her gestures. Apparently romantic audiences were able to see overwrought acting *as* overwrought acting, and still—sometimes, but not always—succumb to its allure. When Miss Pope screamed while performing Jane Shore, according to one poetic account, a critic laughed out loud.[12] And when the eccentric actor Romeo Coutts, famous for playing Romeo in the provinces, was invited to perform at Drury Lane, "many of his speeches elicited laughter and ironical applause." His death scene especially amused the London audience. "The applause was ironically tremendous," the actor Fred Belton wrote. Oblivious to its mocking tenor, Coutts mistook the applause for genuine admiration, and "spreading out a handkerchief to protect his finery, he actually gave his death over again, and the curtain descended amidst cat-calls and convulsive laughter."[13]

Romeo Coutts's audience laughed rudely at points in the play where earlier (or more provincial) audiences had wept. We might conclude that audiences were evolving in such a way that they became more sophisticated and less tolerant of histrionic excess. But this teleological view of theater audience evolution ignores the fact that Siddons's audiences seemed able to recognize the extreme quality of her performances—and still succumb to them. The Cheltenham ladies who were undone by Siddons's Belvidera performance went to the theater expecting "a treat of the ludicrous," but emerged weeping believers in Siddons's particular brand of histrionic excess.[14] Romantic audiences were capable of suspending a cynical view of Siddons's stylized mode of acting, and of surrendering to a more "sincere" response.

The Isabella performance that Inchbald credited with reestablishing the preeminence of tragedy served as an inspiration for Germaine de Staël, who described a Siddons performance of that role in her novel *Corinne*. Corinne, an improvisatrice who has been told her style of performing resembles that of Siddons, goes to see Siddons perform in *Isabella; or, The Fatal Marriage*, and remarks upon her physical grandeur.

"The noblest of actresses in her manners," Staël writes, "Mrs. Siddons loses none of her dignity when she throws herself on the ground."[15] Staël goes on to say of Siddons, "Nothing can fail to be admirable when a deep-seated emotion calls it forth, an emotion rising from the soul's center and dominating the person who feels it even more than those who watch" (340). I loved Staël's sentiment—I wanted to believe that nothing could fail to be admirable when deep-seated emotion called it forth—but when I tried to teach Staël's *Corinne*, my students frowned on the novel's emotional excess. Corinne, the improvisatrice, riffs on her hypersensitivity in a final death song, saying, "Feelings, thoughts, noble perhaps, fruitful perhaps, die out with me, and of all the soul's faculties I hold from nature, the only one that I have practiced fully is the faculty of suffering" (417). In reply, her former suitor Lord Nelvil swoons because he is unable "to withstand the violence of his emotion" (417). When we discussed this scene, my students politely strove to keep straight faces, but I thought I heard one of them snicker.

Chapter Ten

R omantic theatergoers not only enjoyed performances that we would find overwrought, they enjoyed watching these performances over and over and over again. In fact, the intensity of their pleasure seemed to stem partly from the repetition, which allowed for a deep familiarity with the lines and gestures associated with particular plays. We might regard the memories of romantic theatergoers as recording devices that were assisted by the repetition of a familiar repertoire. And serving as a further aide-memoire was the condensation of the romantic theatrical experience to a collection of emotionally, visually, or sonically intense scenes that helped to imprint these plays on the memory. The memorization of these "points" made theatergoing more intensely pleasurable, as audience members anticipated these particular moments, watched them play out, and compared them to versions they had already experienced or even enacted themselves. Star turns became so iconographic that a subgenre of thespian mimicry evolved. "To see Mrs Wells not acting one of the parts made famous by Mrs Siddons or Mrs Abington, but imitating them in those same parts, gave their admirers great delight," writes Charles Beecher Hogan.[1]

One of the most popular of Siddons's points was the statue scene in *The Winter's Tale*. Featuring a supposedly dead Hermione brought back to life, the scene was so popular in the eighteenth century that it was sometimes played on its own as a prelude or coda to other dramas, and by the nineteenth century, it was a reliable crowd pleaser, "a miniature sentimental warhorse," according to Stephen Orgel.[2] The success of the moment seemed to depend on the transformative power of the actress. Fred Belton, recounting the highlights of his career on the stage, fondly recalled Madame Vestris performing in a burlesque that featured a statue "like Hermione in the 'Winter's Tale.'" When he first noticed the actress she appeared "like some ancient washerwoman"—"very feeble [with] a mass of clothes . . . huddled about her in a grotesque fashion."[3] But as she listened for her cue, adjusting the folds of her dress and shaking her hair into form, "the bust began to swell, the eyes to brighten and distend" (90). By the time the curtain rose, "she had placed herself in full attitude" and "realised the ideal of perfect beauty" (90).

According to William Hazlitt, Siddons "acted the painted statue to the life—with true monumental dignity and noble passion."[4] Her skill at deploying frozen moments in tragic scenes served her particularly well as she played a frozen woman. She stood on an elevation of three circular steps, and she "looked the statue, even to literal illusion." While the drapery that covered her hid her lower limbs, "it shewed a beauty of head, neck, shoulders, and arms, that Praxiteles might have studied" (Campbell, *Life of Mrs. Siddons*, 2: 265). Her figure was lit from behind so as to seem, at least to James Boaden, "like one of the muses in profile." Siddons's drapery was "ample in its folds and seemingly stony in texture."[5]

Siddons made the statue scene her own by giving a sudden action of her head as the first gesture of Hermione's reanimation. The movement "absolutely *startled*, as though such a miracle had really vivified the marble."[6] Siddons's Hermione was rendered especially memorable on one occasion when the white muslin robe she was wearing caught on fire. As she later recalled, "Surrounded as I was with muslin, the flame would have run like wildfire," but for the alacrity of a scene man who "most humanely crept on his knees and extinguished it, without my knowing anything of the matter" (Campbell, *Life of Mrs. Siddons*, 2: 268). But even less flammable performances of the scene help us to understand the relationship between voice and gesture.[7] Siddons managed to startle her audience by the sudden action of her head, even though the audience was primed to see the statue move. Gesture and speech reinforced each other, ramping up the intensity of the moment.

Despite the difficulty of converting a live performance into a textual representation, there were a few efforts, well in advance of mechanical recording innovations, to preserve actors' gestures in print, none more impossibly ambitious than Gilbert Austin's 1806 *Chironomia; or, A Treatise on Rhetorical Delivery: Comprehending Many Precepts, Both Ancient and Modern, for the Proper Regulation of the Voice, the Countenance, and Gesture.* Austin set out to produce a language of symbols that would make it possible to represent every action "of an actor throughout the whole drama, and to preserve them for posterity." Austin hoped to mark not only actors' dignified looks, but also their "awkward energies, and so bring into the contemplation of posterity the whole identity of the scene."[8] He wanted to allow actors to learn from prior actors, even if the prior actors had already shuffled off this mortal coil. In the future as envisioned by Austin, the aspiring actor "might light, his talents at the perpetually burning lamps of the dead, and proceed at once by their guidance towards the highest honours of the drama" (287). He sought to make it possible for future generations to witness a facsimile of a dead actor's performance. The novice actor might reproduce an old one, so that the "the transitory blaze" of an actor's fame would no longer be "the subject of just and inevitable regret both to the actor and his historian" (287).

Austin used letters to indicate the position of a body part, combining these symbols in elaborate equations to mark tandem motions. The letter "x," for example, stood for "extended," and, combined with a series of other letters, could signal an arm's full range of movement (359). The first letter conveyed the position of the hand, the second the elevation of the arm, the third the transverse situation of the arm, and the fourth the motion or force of the gesture. By this logic, the notation "phfd" would indicate "prone horizontal forward descending" (the motion of one arm) and could be teamed with other strings of letters that indicated the corresponding movements of other body parts (360). The system was so complicated that an actor attempting to follow it would have to take several minutes to achieve one stance in a performance composed of thousands of distinct poses. And an Austin follower, trying to enact from her desk chair the arm motion "seqn"—supine elevated oblique noting—would swat the air ineffectually. However misguided Austin's scheme, its ingeniousness suggests the strength of the desire to freeze an actor's performance in time and to render it available for replication.

Fig. 12. Siddons illustrations in Gilbert Austin's *Chironomia* (1806), The University of Iowa Libraries.

Austin's *Chironomia* displays him as a fussbudget whose grandiose literary dreams were thwarted by the financial exigencies of book production. He writes regretfully in his preface of having to scale back his illustrations in an effort to keep costs down. "It must be confessed, that this saving of expence to the publication has deprived it of a splendor which it would have derived from the spirited designs first intended for it," he writes, before lamenting in particular the effect of this economizing on his figures of Mrs. Siddons (viii). The Siddons illustrations in the *Chironomia* depict the actress enacting Austin's "complex significant gestures" or "attitudes the most noble and expressive," but they also serve as a catalog of iconic poses from her most famous performances (494) (fig. 12).

Austin calls significant gestures "the great ornament of dramatic exhibition," and he insists that "the performance will be the most brilliant in which they abound most" (496). They are not to be confused with the greater number of actors' gestures that are not significant, but "which are no less necessary, though not so splendid nor imposing" (497). In a similar vein, Dion Boucicault encouraged the aspiring actor to avoid "gesticles," small fidgety gestures that might cause audiences to overlook more significant ones.[9]

Austin preserves one of Siddons's Belvidera poses (fig. 13) in his chart of complex significant gestures, and he describes how stylized movements could telegraph emotion in a precise legible manner. Austin writes, "A slight movement of the head, a look of the eye, a turn of hand, a judicious pause or interruption of gesture, or a change of position in the feet often illuminates the meaning of a passage, and sends it full of light and warmth into the understanding" (497). Austin makes clear that speech and gesture are inextricably intertwined by providing the lines Siddons was speaking when she struck the gestures preserved in his list of complex significant gestures. He notes, for example, that the pose from *Douglas* was assumed by Siddons when she spoke the line "Jehovah's arm snatch'd from the waves and brings to me my son" in Act 3, scene 2. Austin writes, "In the passage from Douglas it is rather difficult to conjecture the moment of the action, because another [gesture] is required also on the word 'son,' but the remainder of the line is necessary to complete the sense, and the action seems properly placed on 'Jehova's arm.'" He observes that the gesture depicted for *Venice Preserved* (kneeling, one hand to forehead) should be struck at the end of the phrase "pity and forgiveness," and preceded by a different gesture on the word "pity": "The head cast down, and *both hands clasped elevated forwards* significant of the profound humility implied in the word 'pity'" (496).

Siddons's gestures seem to have been inordinately expressive, and so helped her to create points that audience members could easily preserve in memory. Fanny Kemble noted her aunt's majesty stillness of

Fig. 13. Detail of Belvidera in *Chironomia* (1806), The University of Iowa Libraries.

manner, and nearly every literary critic or theater historian who has written about Siddons's performances has commented on her magisterial stage presence, most evident in moments of silence.[10] William Hazlitt called Siddons a "pantomime actress"; the power of her speeches was partly derived from the power of her gestures.[11] "In many roles, she would stop the action in a 'frozen moment' of deliberation before breaking into an outburst of grief or frenzy," writes Frederick Burwick.[12] James Boaden, too, praised her strategic use of the sustained pause: "In the hurry of distraction she could stop, and in some frenzied attitude speak wonders to the eye, till a second rush forward brought her to the proper ground on which her utterance might be trusted" (*Memoirs of Mrs. Siddons*, 2: 289). Her star turn as Queen Katherine in *Henry VIII*—the performance that led Joseph Severn to discover his calling—derived much of its power from accusatory gestures.[13]

Siddons dazzled theatergoers when she first performed as Hermione in 1802, but also when she reprised the role in 1807 and 1811. A reviewer for the *Times* declared that Siddons's 1802 interpretation of Hermione "towered beyond all praise."[14] "Whatever Hermione is," a reviewer for the *Morning Chronicle* concurred in 1807, "Mrs Siddons has made her; creation is the power which has raised this great actress to lofty pre-eminence."[15] "She rose to divinity in the statue scene," proclaimed the *Antigallican Monitor* in 1811.[16]

Siddons was, by all accounts, an impressive female specimen, a little large-nosed ("Damn the nose—there's no end to it," Thomas Gainsborough complained),[17] and beginning to lose her figure by the time she performed Hermione, but a handsome woman with an expressive face. The fascination with her static figure was matched by a fascination with Siddons's vocal performance. She "gave to the lines of Shakespeare an energy and fascination of which no other actress was capable," wrote a reviewer of her 1802 Hermione.[18]

Siddons's voice combined with Siddons's gestures proved too forceful for some audience members. Queen Charlotte turned her back on the stage when Siddons's acting made it difficult for her to maintain her royal sangfroid. Charlotte could bear listening to Siddons at her most intense as long as she wasn't seeing her at the same time. And when Siddons played Mrs. Beverley in *The Gamester*, some of her admirers watched through the square glasses of the box doors, "so as not to hear the words, but only see the wonderful face."[19] For the people standing outside the box doors, Siddons was performing Mrs. Beverley by semaphore. They were watching only her gestures, which were extensive and, arguably, as expressive as her intonations.[20]

In John Philip Kemble's adaptation of the play's most famous scene, Hermione's first speech upon reanimation inspires her husband, Leontes, to comment on the quality of her voice past and present. "Hark, hark, she speaks!" Leontes exclaims, before going on to remark, "O, pipe, through sixteen winters dumb! then deem'd / Harsh as the raven's throat; now musical / As nature's song, tun'd to the according spheres."[21] The line conjured Lady Macbeth's famous soliloquy: "The raven himself is hoarse / That croaks the fatal entrance of Duncan / Under my battlements. Come, you spirits / That tend on mortal thoughts, unsex me here, / And fill me from the crown to the toe, top-full / Of direst cruelty."[22] One Siddons performance set off reverbera-tions of another; Siddons as Hermione activated the harmonic echo of Siddons as Lady Macbeth. Siddons also managed to haunt stage char-acters that most people had never seen her perform.

Chapter Eleven

It's possible there was no stage role more familiar to romantic the-atergoers than Hamlet. Romantic era theater audiences were swimming in Hamlets, recalling how *Hamlet* lines were spoken by prior Hamlets, and inflating these memories whenever a brash tradition-flouting Hamlet roiled the water.[1] So, for example, when Siddons's brother John Philip Kemble, while performing that role, said "*un-weeded*" instead of "*un*-weeded," and "Did *you* not speak to it?" instead of "Did you not *speak* to it?", it did not go unnoted.[2] Many of Kemble's audience members heard in their heads the Hamlet of David Garrick, who dispensed with a static declamatory manner of speaking lines, and substituted rapid changes of voice and gesture that seemed entirely natural even though he wore a fright wig so that Hamlet's hair would stand on end when he encountered his father's ghost.

In selecting *Hamlet* for his 1783 debut, Kemble opted for the people's choice of Shakespeare play. Kemble declared, "Take up any Shakespeare you will, from the first collection of his works to the last, which has been *read*, and look what play bears the most obvious signs of perusal. My life for it, they will be found in the volume which contains the play of Hamlet." And he backed this assertion up with his own data-base, going on to state, "I dare say, in my time, some hundred copies have been inspected by me; but this test has never failed in a single instance."[3] He overprepared for the role with a similar obsessiveness, copying and recopying his lines as he tinkered with the part, so that when his friend John Taylor suggested he make some changes, Kemble protested, "Now, Taylor, I have copied the part of Hamlet forty times, and you have obliged me to consider and copy it once more."[4] Given that Kemble was capable of reciting fifteen hundred lines of Homer from memory, and, along with Siddons, rose to the task of memorizing the lines of the still-being-written *Pizarro*, as the play was being performed, his painstaking approach to learning his Hamlet part is all the more striking.[5]

Kemble prepared with the ghost of Garrick hanging over his shoulder and, quite possibly, with Garrick's copy of the play on his desk. Garrick's eccentric alteration of the play had its own ghostly reputation. Rumored to have been buried with the actor, it was actually given to Kemble as a curiosity from Mrs. Garrick, who also presented the cane Garrick used to walk abroad, a cane that Kemble quickly regifted.[6] But when Kemble stepped on stage at Drury Lane, the actor he conjured was Siddons, not Garrick. As Boaden recalled, "On Mr. Kemble's first appearance before the spectators, the general exclamation was, 'How very like his sister!' and there was a very striking resemblance."[7] According to a review in the *Morning Chronicle*, his voice "in some of its tones [sounded] so like that of his sister, that were a blind person, familiar to the voice of Mrs. Siddons, to hear Mr. Kemble speak, he might mistake the one for the other."[8] When Kemble debuted his Hamlet at Drury Lane, Siddons had only played that role in the provinces; the audience wasn't seeing and hearing Siddons when they watched Kemble play Hamlet because they'd already seen and heard her do it, but because his melancholy manner recalled hers as she performed many other tragic roles. "His person seemed to be finely formed, and his manners princely; but on his brow hung the weight of 'some intolerable woe,'" Boaden wrote (*Kemble*, 1: 92). The Gothic novelist Ann Radcliffe, who may or may not have seen Siddons as Hamlet—Radcliffe's biographer speculates that she saw Siddons perform the role at the Bath-Bristol Theatre-Royal—supposed that Siddons would be the finest Hamlet that ever appeared, finer even than her brother. "She would more fully preserve the tender and refined melancholy," Radcliffe wrote, "the deep sensibility, which are the peculiar charm of Hamlet, and which appear not only in the ardour, but in the occasional irresolution and weakness of his character—the secret spring that reconciles all his inconsistencies."[9] Radcliffe attributed

Kemble's lesser ability to play Hamlet to a firmness "incapable of being always subdued," and claimed Siddons's tenderness, by contrast, would serve to enhance Hamlet's sensibility, a sensibility "so profound [it can only] with difficulty be justly imagined, and therefore can very rarely be assumed" (147).

Siddons most famously performed Hamlet just a few months after she introduced Hermione to her London repertoire, but not for the first time.[10] Of Siddons's entire Hamlet performance history, we have little documentation, mostly just a pieced-together roster of provincial performance dates. We know that she played Hamlet "to the satisfaction of the Worcester critics" sometime in 1775, that she reprised the role in Manchester on 19 March 1778, with her brother playing Laertes, and that she took the role to Liverpool sometime that same year. We can date her second Birmingham appearance as Hamlet to 19 March 1777, and we can confirm that she played the role in Bath the year after. She played Hamlet in Bristol in 1781, and then she either stopped playing Hamlet for twenty years, or else the historical record of her later performances has been lost. She finally reprised the title role in Dublin on 27 July 1802, when she was forty-seven years old, overweight, and suffering from voice strain.[11] That Siddons could be effective in a role for which she was so physically unsuited underscores yet again how important her voice was to her manifestation of characters. Through her auditory rather than her physical presentation she managed to credibly impersonate a young man, and to do so in a way that didn't seem like a mere impersonation.

Unfortunately, the voice Siddons used to speak the lines of Hamlet is even more elusive than the voice Siddons used to speak the lines of other roles. The most vivid surviving traces of her Hamlet performances are glimpses of the costume and actions she adopted for the role. This should not be surprising, because even though the way Siddons sounded as Hamlet stuck in audience members' long-term memories and led them to suggest that a blind person might mistake Kemble for his sister when Kemble played the same role, the way Siddons looked and behaved during her Dublin Hamlet run provoked short-term gossip and scandalous speculation.

It's curious that the image-conscious actress played Hamlet at all, given the expectation that Hamlet would dress in male clothing. To play Rosalind, Siddons reportedly wore "something like a gardener's apron in front and a petticoat behind" so as to avoid wearing breeches.[12] Siddons was not the only woman to play the role, even in her own day, but the other female Hamlets were less concerned about public rectitude.

Charlotte Charke, in her 1755 memoir, recalled playing Hamlet in the provinces out of expediency, for lack of a suitable man to play the role. But Charke had already made a career out of flouting conventions, cross-dressing so that she could work as a waiter, a proofreader, and a sausage maker.[13] Jane Powell, who sometimes substituted for Siddons at Drury Lane, took on a number of male roles—Norval in *Douglas*, Douglas in *Douglas*, and Hamlet on several occasions—but Powell (née Palmer, then Mrs. Farmer, then Mrs. Renaud) had a busy sexual past and was less concerned about how playing male roles might harm her reputation. When Powell played Douglas, there was nothing halfheartedly masculine about her clothing, and when she played Hamlet "she looked the character remarkably well; that is, according to the *general idea*."[14]

Siddons, by contrast, played Hamlet despite the costuming requirement, or at least that's what she wanted people to think. When she played the role in Dublin in 1802, she wrapped herself in what looked like a fringed blanket that covered her from knees to ruffly collar, and she topped herself off with a plumed hat and a cross necklace. A sword hung from her side, but it's hard to imagine how she could have lunged in the fencing scene without getting tangled up in her cape.

Mary Hamilton's watercolor rendition of Siddons's Hamlet costume, part of a series of sketches she drew of Siddons in scenes from her Dublin performances, is carefully labeled "Mrs. Siddons's Dress as Hamlet. Act Ist, Scene II: 'Aye Madam, it is common'" (fig. 14). The drawing apparently evokes how Siddons looked as she delivered the line Hamlet speaks after Gertrude tells him to cast his nightly color off since all that live must die. Why did Hamilton sketch Siddons as she spoke this line of all others, we're left to wonder? Hamlet's response to his mother, "Aye Madam, it is common," takes the form of a rebuke. Standing on stage in quasi-masculine clothing, Siddons accused Gertrude of sexual impropriety at the very moment when she was rendering herself vulnerable to the same accusation by playing Hamlet.

Mary Hamilton left her caped figure faceless, making it look like Siddons stepped out for a minute while her clothes stood waiting for her. The drawing serves as a metaphor for the surviving accounts of

Fig. 14. Mary Sackville Hamilton, *Sarah Siddons as Hamlet* (1805),
© Trustees of the British Museum.

Siddons's Hamlet, which tend to be missing what is for us the most in-accessible feature of the actual performances, the way she sounded while playing the role.

The main trace of Siddons's Dublin Hamlet performance survives in *Mrs. Galindo's Letter to Mrs. Siddons,* a resentful screed penned by the wife of Siddons's fencing instructor. Mr. Galindo was a success as Siddons's fencing partner—he played Laertes to her Hamlet, and their swordplay won praise.[15] But according to his wife, the two teamed up romantically as well. Suspicious of an affair, Mrs. Galindo tracked Siddons's every move with the tenaciousness of a surveillance device. She describes how Siddons had Mr. Galindo drive her around Dublin in his curricle, and how, when Siddons took sick, she insisted that only Mr. Galindo attend her.[16] She recalls the time Siddons got Mr. Galindo to accompany her to the spring assizes in Cork, and she provides a bookkeeper's breakdown of how much this trip cost (12).

Published seven years after the performance took place, Catherine Galindo's *Letter* constructs Siddons's Dublin Hamlet performance as a ploy to enable sexual impropriety. Addressing Siddons, she writes, "About this period you proposed to Mr. Jones to perform Hamlet, I now believe for no other purpose than to be taught *fencing* by Mr. G. for by so doing you had an excuse to have him constantly with you, to the exclusion of my company, as you said you could not be instructed while any person looked on" (7–8) (fig. 15) And there may be some truth to Galindo's accusation—not necessarily in the suggestion that Siddons was set on stealing her husband, but rather in the implication that Siddons was keen on being taught fencing, which must have seemed inordinately exciting to a middle-aged woman whose physical assets were shrinking.

Serious fencers are careful to make a distinction between actual fencing and stage fencing, and, in fact, speak dismissively of stage fencing in the same manner that a professional ballet dancer might talk about a person who pirouettes around the kitchen when she plays her *Nutcracker* CD. Still, anyone who takes up fencing as a middle-aged person will sympathize with Siddons's experience, especially if her experience included spending an uncomfortable amount of time with her knees flexed in a position aimed at keeping the fencer's body close to the ground and the fencer ready to spring, leaving an older fencer to wonder when her knees are going to pop and provide a legitimate excuse to watch from the sidelines.

For the novice fencer, crouching is followed by lunging, a complicated maneuver that involves thrusting the arm to a fully extended position just in advance of changing the legs from the painful deep-bend position to a slightly less painful, but even more potentially cartilage-damaging lunge position. Siddons must have had to learn some variant of this move because whether you are an actual fencer or merely play-

Fig. 15. Mrs. Siddons giving Mr. Galindo a stab to the heart (ca. 1802), Thr 489.3.29, Harvard Theatre Collection, Houghton Library, Harvard University.

ing one on stage, this is the move that defines the fencing combatant. We have no way of knowing exactly how Siddons mastered or failed to master this maneuver, since, as Catherine Galindo balefully attests, Siddons allowed no visitors to her training session. So we don't know how successful Siddons was at carrying out the arm thrust just a half beat before she stepped into a fully extended lunge. Nor do we know whether Mr. Galindo and Siddons took turns lunging at each other and jabbing each other in the chest with the points of their weapons, as present-day fencing students are encouraged to do in a drill that causes bruises to bloom on one's upper torso.

It doesn't seem unreasonable that Siddons insisted that no one look on while she was taking fencing lessons, given that the gracefulness of the experienced fencer, who zips back and forth in a light-footed pas de chat, comes only after many weeks of galumphing back and forth with a rhinoceros footfall that has no dance parallel. No, no, there's nothing graceful about a fencer who hasn't mastered the footwork, so you can't blame Siddons for not wanting anyone to see her, all flex-kneed and awkward, trying to mirror Mr. Galindo's moves.

Catherine Galindo claims that Mr. Galindo dined with Mrs. Siddons constantly and often spent the night, and she accuses Siddons of writing to her husband "in a FALSE ALPHABET" (34). The capital lettering urges you to feel Mrs. Galindo's pain, as does her address to "a public, ever ready to hear with candour the complaints of the oppressed" (34). She asks, "Should the mother of three innocent, and *yet infant children*, crouch under such accumulated wrongs and not seek for redress?" (34). She then rises from her crouch, and in a rhetorical move that might be likened to a fencer's "fleche" attack, in which one lunges at one's opponent with foil extended and keeps on running right past, she describes an occasion when Mrs. S. and Mr. G. were taking the air in the Galindo family curricle. Mrs. Galindo, addressing Siddons directly, writes, "From *some reasons* you and he thought fit to stop and put up the head of the carriage" (39). Mrs. Galindo goes on to describe the party of ladies and gentlemen who, seeing a carriage standing still, thought an accident had occurred, and who saw "to their great surprize that instead of their assistance being required, they had been guilty of a most mal-a-propos intrusion" (40).

It's possible that the bodily freedom Siddons experienced while taking fencing lessons lured her into taking other bodily liberties, and even though Mrs. Galindo's *Letter* is not entirely trustworthy, the glimpse she provides of Siddons's preparation to play Hamlet provides a means of contextualizing what seems like a peculiar career choice.

With Siddons, perhaps, as her role model, Sarah Bernhardt also played Hamlet; in fact, she went so far as to suggest that Hamlet was best played by women rather than men, because a woman, presumably even a middle-aged woman, was better suited to portray a youth of twenty or twenty-one with the mind of a man of forty.[17] But Siddons, unlike Bernhardt, didn't look like a youth of twenty when she played Hamlet, and her fans (and her main foe) did a remarkably poor job of chronicling one of the most ambitious physical and vocal performances of her career. Why, oh why, couldn't Catherine Galindo have paused in her scandal-mongering to describe the timbre of Siddons's voice when she spoke Hamlet's soliloquy? Why did Ann Radcliffe, the queen of attenuated description, a novelist who never met a forest glen whose murky shadow did not merit a lengthy digression, fail to describe how Siddons sounded when she spoke "The rest is silence," Hamlet's final line?

Ann Radcliffe provides the most detailed analysis of Siddons in this role, but her musings on Siddons's Hamlet occur during a discussion of the sublime, and so they tail off into a landscape comparison. "The strong light which shows the mountains of a landscape in all their greatness, and with all their rugged sharpnesses," Radcliffe writes, "gives them nothing of the interest with which a more gloomy tint would invest their grandeur; dignifying, though it softens, and magnifying, while it obscures" (147). Siddons's Hamlet is to her brother's Hamlet, in Radcliffe's assessment, as moonlight is to sunlight on a mountain range, a visual analogy that provides no certain knowledge of how either actor sounded.

"Why can't he learn from his sister," George Joseph Bell sighed years later, commenting on a Kemble performance. Bell went on to recall how Siddons "in reading 'Hamlet' showed how inimitably she could by a mere look, while sitting in a chair, paint to the spectators a horrible shadow in her mind."[18] Bell references the stripped-down version of Hamlet that would have been possible for an actor reading while sitting in a chair, a version that, of course, would have drawn attention to her voice even more than the stage version. Siddons resorted to this kind of audio-showcasing format with increasing frequency late in her career.

Chapter Twelve

If we want to judge what role Siddons's voice played in creating the Siddons phenomenon, the transfixing and traumatizing of audience members, we must look at the series of public readings she gave across the length of her career. Before the king and queen at Frogmore, in an assembly room in Dublin, and in the Argyle public room in London, Siddons read passages from Shakespeare's plays and from *Paradise Lost*, enacting all the characters, rather than just the ones she played on stage. In the best visual record we have of a Siddons reading, Thomas Lawrence's 1804 portrait (fig. 16), Siddons looks as impenetrable as a fortress. Her body a black velvet tower, she stands next to a book that is big enough to contain wallpaper samples, and plucks one giant page as she stares impassively at the audience. The painting conveys neither the dynamism of her readings nor the varied responses that they elicited. "She acted Macbeth himself better than either Kemble or Kean," Benjamin Robert Haydon wrote of one Siddons reading, going on to say, "It is extraordinary the awe this wonderful woman inspires."[1] But the readings led others to decamp from the Siddons fan club, and to complain that she had become a stilted and pretentious version of herself.

Siddons was not the only person giving readings of one kind or another in early nineteenth-century London. In early 1818, William Hazlitt spoke on English poets; Coleridge lectured on "the *Belles-Lettres*"; John Thelwall expounded on poetry, the drama, and elocution;

Fig. 16. Sir Thomas Lawrence, *Mrs Siddons* (1804), The Tate Gallery/
Digital Image © Tate, London 2009.

and a Mr. Webster discussed steam.[2] Siddons was also not the first actor to venture out on the reading circuit—John Henderson capitalized on his supple voice by giving Shakespeare readings.[3] Nor would she be the last reader to enact a wide range of characters—Charles Dickens's harrowing readings of Nancy's murder in *Oliver Twist* reportedly hastened his own death.[4] But as a renowned actor giving pared-down versions of her stage performances *and* as a woman reading male parts, she was using her voice in new and perilous circumstances.

One account of a Siddons reading is preserved in a single sentence of *Mrs. Galindo's Letter to Mrs. Siddons*, which refers, briefly and tantalizingly, to the time when Siddons was "reading Paradise Lost at the Lying-in-Hospital rooms, and had engaged to give the last night's receipt to the charity" (12).[5] *Paradise Lost* may seem like an odd choice of reading material for a lying-in hospital, but, from an early age, Siddons was smitten with Milton's epic, and it assumed an important place in her public readings. There survives in the Harvard library Siddons's manuscript copy of *Paradise Lost*, prefaced by a handwritten announcement that the poem was "abridged at the request of some friends, for the purpose of dividing it into four readings."[6]

I spent a day collating Siddons's reading copy of Milton's poem, which includes frequent underlining, seemingly aimed at reminding her where to place emphasis. When she transcribed "impious war in Heavn, and battle proud," she underlined "war." When she copied Milton's description of Satan and his horrid crew rolling in the fiery gulph, she underlined the words "more wrath," in the line "But his doom / Reserved him to more wrath," as if to stop herself from lapsing into an iamb. It is possible to determine from the *Paradise Lost* manuscript Sarah Siddons's pattern of omissions, to ascertain that she cut a great swath from the opening of Book IX, so that she could get straight to the business of Eve convincing Adam that they should divide their labors.[7] It is far harder to figure out how she sounded when she read any of Milton's lines. Although her underlining almost certainly serves as a cue for emphasis, and she seems to use an "x" in the margin to mark an omission, the series of small circles she drew under parts of certain lines, rows of tiny inflated dots of the kind adolescent girls use to dot "i"s, is harder to parse. Under Milton's lines, "What in me is dark / Illumine, what is low raise and support," Siddons drew one of these strings of beads, signifying something that her audience must have heard as a shift in her reading, a slowing down for emphasis, perhaps. The dots do not correspond to syllables in the lines, but perhaps they draw her attention to a string of monosyllables she didn't want to rush.[8]

When Siddons began reading "Of Man's first disobedience, and the fruit / Of that forbidden tree, whose mortal taste / Brought Death into the world, and all our woe" at the Dublin hospital, she likely did so in a large "Rotundo" where the hospital held organ recitals and other concerts in an effort to raise funds. When Mrs. Galindo mentions Siddons reading in the lying-in hospital "rooms," she is likely referring to the kind of rooms Jane Austen conjures when her characters go to the Assembly Rooms at Bath, and not to the wards where women were laboring or convalescing nearby.

Audience responses to that reading do not survive, but the responses to other Siddons readings in more intimate spaces suggest that Siddons's majestic aura dissipated a little when she stepped out of the theater, that the grandeur of the playhouse reinforced or supported the grandeur of her vocalizations. After performing for the royal family at Frogmore, Siddons wrote, "It all went off to my heart's content, for the room was the finest place for the voice in the world."[9] When, on a subsequent evening, she read for the queen passages from *Paradise Lost*, Gray's "Elegy," and Scott's *Marmion*, or when she was called back days later for a command reading of *Othello*, she could count on a respectful audience.[10] But when Frances Burney met Siddons after one of her readings for the royal family, she was "much disappointed in [her] expectations."[11]

Burney's objection to Siddons lay partly in the actress's failure to modulate between stage oration and ordinary conversation. "I found her the Heroine of a Tragedy," Burney wrote, as if to say she wasn't pleased to encounter Lady Macbeth or Queen Katherine in a drawing room.[12] The barrister Thomas Erskine said Siddons's performance was a school for orators, crediting his "best displays" to his emulation of "the harmony of her periods and pronunciation," but she failed to reserve her dramatic tones for the stage (Campbell, *Life of Mrs. Siddons*, 2: 381). She once startled a Mercer in Bath with her habit of attaching dramatic tones to ordinary subjects. After hearing the cloth salesman list the virtues of a bolt of calico, she spoke the question, "*But will it wash?*" in a manner "so electrifying as to make the poor shopman start back from his counter" (2: 393). When Siddons unsheathed her voice in the fabric store or at the tea table, the result could be inadvertently comic. It was like hearing Pavarotti count change or Ethel Merman make small talk.[13]

Others responded more equivocally to Siddons reading. When Joanna Baillie heard her read at the Argyle Rooms in 1813, she praised her *Hamlet* reading but thought it compared unfavorably to a *Macbeth* reading she'd heard a few weeks before. She admired Hamlet's first soliloquy as delivered by Siddons, but went on to write, "There were frequent bursts of voice beyond what natural passion warranted and in no good keeping (to use a painter's term) with the general tone of the whole which annoyed me a good deal."[14] Baillie insisted on calling what Siddons was doing acting rather than reading, claiming that she relied too heavily on "countenance & gesture," but conceding that if she didn't rely on these acting skills, "however she might delight her friends in private, she could not night after night fill a public room." However, Baillie still wrote mournfully that when Siddons's performances would cease, "*we* of this generation can never look to see the like again." And she ended her comments on Siddons by saying that she would rather go to one of her readings "than go to three plays in a large Theatre where she herself acted."

Baillie's comments suggest that Siddons's reading performances were a little too much for the venue, and possibly tainted by the style of big acting that had allowed her to maintain her impact on stage even as she was increasingly dwarfed by large theaters and spectacular effects. But as she got older, and, possibly, as the disconnect between her aging body and the myriad roles she read grew larger, her performances at times grew inadvertently comic. Of her ill-advised return to the stage in 1816, four years after her official retirement, Joseph Roach writes, "Slow of speech and largely immobile, she now exhibited vulnerabilities that so surpassed her strengths that by coming again upon the boards she risked the almost certain destruction of her hard-won image as an 'idol' in the public mind."[15] A caricature of "the rival queens of Covent Garden" presents an unflattering depiction of a rotund Siddons gesticulating alongside a svelte and elegant Eliza O'Neill, who was Siddons's junior by thirty-six years (fig. 17).

Haydon, who witnessed Siddons reading from *Macbeth* in 1821, leaves the most vivid account of her voice's fraught circumstances. He writes, "After her first reading the men sallied into a room to get Tea. While we were all eating toast & tingling cups & saucers, she began

Fig. 17. Charles Williams, *Theatrical jealousy, or, the rival queens of Covent Garden* (1816), By Permission of The Folger Shakespeare Library.

again. Immediately like the effect of a mass bell at Madrid, all noise ceased, and we slunk away to our seats like boys, two or three of the most distinguished men of the day passed me to get to their seats with great bits of toast sticking out their cheeks, which they seemed afraid to bite" (*Diary*, 2: 310). Haydon goes on to describe the painter Thomas Lawrence, one of Siddons's most devoted admirers, caught with his mouth full. "It was curious suddenly to look up & see Lawrence's face pass you in the bustle with his cheek swelled from his mouth being full," Haydon writes, "and then when he sat down, hearing him bite it by degrees, & then stop for fear of making too much crackle, while his eyes full of water told the torture he was in; at the same moment you heard Mrs Siddons say 'Eye of newt, toe of frog'; then Lawrence gave a bite & pretended to be awed & listening" (2: 310–11). Haydon exited the performance "highly gratified," but as he paused on a landing place, he overheard servants speaking. Haydon writes, "While upstairs we were awed & Mrs. Siddons was talking like a Pythoness, a Servant says,

94

'is that the old Lady making such a noise!' It awakened me out of a
Dream, and made one think perhaps that the old Lady *was* making a
noise" (2: 311).

Perhaps the final and most poignant record of a Siddons reading is
provided by Joanna Baillie, who heard her read *Hamlet* again at a dinner party a year before Siddons's death. Baillie expected to see "much
decay in her powers of expression, and consequently to have [her] pleasure mingled with pain."[16] Baillie recalls how Siddons complained
about her voice, which she said was no longer obedient to her will, but
in Baillie's view Siddons's voice had improved with age "because it had
lost that deep solemnity of tone which she, perhaps, had considered as
an excellence." Siddons's reading of a *Hamlet* scene touched Baillie's
heart "as it had never done before," and inspired another guest to regret that those who were there to hear it were not young enough to
have their memories serve as recordings as long as might have been
possible.[17] A Mr. Rogers said, "Oh, that we could have assembled a
company of young people to witness this, that they might have conveyed the memory of it down to another generation!" He saw the gathered company as a coterie of recording devices that would all too soon
grow obsolete.

Chapter Thirteen

O ver the course of my research, I consulted a farrago of alluring Siddons artifacts. I handled Siddons's fragile copy of *Cymbeline*, which revealed that she had only one page to change into her night dress for the bed chamber scene. I looked over the seating chart for one of Siddons's readings, and I examined the list of signatories on a petition to coax Siddons back onto the stage. I studied the auction catalog that lists Siddons's household remains, and I skimmed Siddons's prayer book, wondering about the great-great-grand-daughter who, in 1928, had sold it. But nothing seemed as promising as the notes taken by George Joseph Bell while he was sitting in Siddons's audience, notes that have been bound in three leather volumes, and that are now in the holdings of the Folger Shakespeare Library.

George Joseph Bell seems, at first glance, an unlikely chronicler of Siddons's star turns. Born the third son of a Scottish Episcopal clergyman in 1770, he made his notes on Siddons around 1809, by which time he was known as the author of a treatise on the laws of bankruptcy in Scotland. However, Bell's status as a recorder of Siddons's vocal nuances accords well with the combined artistic and scientific propensities of his family members. Bell's older brother John, a surgeon and anatomist, opened his own lecture theater in Edinburgh and drew the illustrations for his treatise *The Anatomy of the Bones, Muscles, and Joints* (1793–94). George Joseph Bell's younger brother Charles was a physiologist and surgeon whose 1806 *Anatomy of Expression* attempted to explain the anatomical basis for the artistic representation of emotion. Charles Bell's lectures on anatomy attracted artists as well as medical students. All three brothers were lecturers; George Joseph Bell may have had a professional as well as a recreational interest in the way in which Siddons declaimed her lines.

Bell's notes stand as one point on a trajectory of efforts to create a written recording of the voice in advance of the moment when a phonograph stylus would "write" the vibrations of the voice onto a wax cylinder. George Joseph Bell was possibly a relative of Alexander Bell (1790–1865), a Shakespeare scholar and public reader of Shakespeare's plays, who insisted that his famous grandson, the inventor Alexander Graham Bell, memorize great swaths of Shakespeare's plays, including passages from *Macbeth*. Alexander Graham Bell's father, Alexander Melville Bell, devised an alphabet for recording the sounds of all languages, and enlisted his son to serve as his assistant when he gave public lectures on his system of Universal Alphabetics. While the young Bell was out of the room, audience members were encouraged to make strange sounds that Bell senior translated into this system of symbols. When Alexander Graham Bell would return to the hall, he would, on the basis of his father's notations, reproduce a sound that he had never heard. The younger Bell recalled, "I remember upon one occasion the attempt to follow directions resulted in a curious rasping noise that was utterly unintelligible to me. The audience, however, at once responded with loud applause. They recognized it as an imitation of the noise of sawing wood, which had been given by an amateur ventriloquist as a test."[1] John Durham Peters writes, "This is the primal scene of the supercession of presence by programming."[2]

Bell made his notes in the margins of published plays. He devoted his most detailed note-taking to Siddons's performance in *Macbeth*, which is understandable, given the acclaim she received for that role and the many times she reprised it over the course of her career.[3] Siddons took over the role of Lady Macbeth from the celebrated Hannah Pritchard and made it her own by putting down her candle in the sleep-walking scene—a startling break from stage tradition. When John Philip Kemble became acting manager of the Drury Lane theater, he began regularly performing the role of Macbeth alongside his sister, and, in 1794, Kemble opened the newly rebuilt theater with a spectacular production of *Macbeth* that included a large chorus, rolling thunder, and flying witches. When Kemble moved to the Covent Garden theater in 1803, *Macbeth* was staged seven times that season, and every season after to the end of his career. (The play was also used for the opening of the rebuilt Covent Garden theater in 1809.) Sarah Siddons played Lady Macbeth nine times during her 1811–12 farewell season, and the role occasionally lured her out of retirement.[4]

One of the reasons why the play provided such a showcase for Siddons's vocal powers is that it takes the female voice as a subject of fascination from its very first scene. *Macbeth* opens with the gathering of witches whose gnomic observations set the course of the events that follow. Their vocal exoticism was highlighted in John Philip Kemble's version of the play; cat and toad sounds were conveyed from stage right and stage left in advance of the witches' scripted responses to their unseen animals ("I come, Gray-malkin" and "Paddock calls").[5] (That the ostensibly female witches were played by male actors also drew attention to the oddity of their voices.) Lady Macbeth, too, conjures up an animal voice when she anticipates the arrival of the king in Act I by saying, "The raven himself is hoarse, / That croaks the fatal entrance of Duncan."[6]

I didn't have to visit the Folger Shakespeare Library to examine Bell's notes. His comments on Siddons in the role of Lady Macbeth (and also in the role of Queen Katherine) were transcribed and published in 1878 by H. C. Fleeming Jenkin (1833–85), an electrical engineer who worked on the development of the telegraph cable, and who was immortalized in Robert Louis Stevenson's essay "Talk and Talkers." Jenkin's transcription was reprinted by the Dramatic Museum of Columbia University in a drab cloth binding as part of a series entitled "Papers on Acting."

I had been monopolizing a library copy of the Bell transcription since the beginning of my Siddons sojourn. From Jenkin's publication, I learned that Bell began his commentary on Siddons by describing Lady Macbeth's first words after she enters reading Macbeth's letter. When Siddons spoke the line, "Glamis thou art, and Cawdor, *and shalt be,* / What thou art promis'd," she did so in an "exalted prophetic tone, as if the whole future were present to her soul." Bell added that she displayed "a slight tincture of contempt throughout."[7] At the opening of Act III, scene 2, when Siddons spoke the line, "Is Banquo gone from court?" Bell noted that she did so with "great dignity and solemnity of voice; nothing of the joy of gratified ambition" (57). A few lines later, Lady Macbeth says, "Nought's had, all's spent, / Where our desire is got without content: / 'Tis safer to be that which we destroy / Than by destruction dwell in doubtful joy." In Siddons's delivery, the lines were "very mournful" (57). Jenkin's transcript faithfully records that Bell used slash marks to indicate the rise or fall of Siddons's voice, and underlining to mark words she spoke with special emphasis. It also preserves Bell's observation that when she spoke the line, "One, two, why, then 'tis time to do't," she did so in a "strange unnatural whisper" (67). And that when she spoke "The thane of Fife had a wife," she used a "very melancholy tone" (67). When she emitted her final sigh, "Oh, oh, oh!" according to Bell, it was not a sigh, but rather "a convulsive shudder—very horrible," with "a tone of imbecility" (68).

Over the course of my research I had turned to Jenkin's transcript of Bell's notes many times, sometimes using it as a coaster on which to perch cups of tea, sometimes making of it a dead weight in order to wedge open larger books with tight bindings, and sometimes studying its pages with a keen eye since it was the closest thing I had to a Siddons MP3. But even though Jenkin had been the faithful companion of my Siddons pursuits, I had always hoped that he was a careless transcriber, that when he was transporting notes from the margins of the play texts on which Bell did his scribbling to a press-ready typescript, he had neglected to convey Bell's comments in their entirety. I believed that if I could study Bell's comments in their original format, I would discover some small but crucial aperçu that Jenkin had neglected to transcribe.

However, when I finally made a pilgrimage to the Folger Library and examined Bell's notes in their original format, Jenkin's lapses did not reveal themselves.[8] In fact, his transcription seemed remarkably close to the original, and much easier to read. Nevertheless, I was grateful to carry away from the Folger a digitized replica of a microfilm version of Bell's original notes for future inspection. I could not have imagined that upon arriving home I would shove the Bell CD in a manila folder reserved for photo requests and let it rest there so long that it turned into an archaic storage device, since the laptop that replaced the one I carried to the Folger Library didn't have an internal CD drive.

When I finally downloaded the CD contents, I learned that the Bell microfilm scroll begins with a microphoto of a Folger catalog card. Back in the heyday of typewriters, a librarian had carefully described the volume of *The British Theatre* that Bell had annotated, and below her typed bibliographic entry there was appended a neat handwritten notice that Bell's comments are referenced in *Macbeth and the Players*, by D. Bartholomeusz, who erroneously attributes them to Prof. John Bell. The librarians who had penned updates and corrections on catalog cards were now straightening the bookshelves at retirement homes if they weren't already dead. Their voices, carefully modulated in life, could now only be accessed through microscript annotations.

In the spirit of those librarians, though, I noticed that Jenkin transcribed "throughout" as "thruout," and that he was reckless in his insertion of commas where Bell used dashes, or where Bell used no punctuation at all. But mostly Jenkin turned out to be a scrupulous copyist. He did not overlook any of Bell's Lady Macbeth observations, but those observations seemed more revealing when, because I was trying to catch Jenkin in an error, I read them at snail speed. I noticed for the first time how fully Bell reported on reactions to Siddons's acting, and how he did so in the second person, writing that her anxiety in the banquet scene "makes you creep with apprehension," and that her emotion "keeps you breathless" (62). And though I was breathing in my usual shallow manner, I paused over his description of how Siddons spoke her last big speech in scene 5 of Act I, because that was the speech I had used in my "Voice for Actors" class to practice breathing exercises.

The Bell marginalia mostly reinforced what I had already learned. I was different from Bell—I was different from nearly all of Siddons's fans—because I didn't carry her voice in my head, but I was also different from her fans because I wasn't familiar with all of her lines. Thomas Love Peacock claimed he had heard Shelley read "almost all Shakespeare's tragedies, and some of his more poetical comedies," and that "it was a pleasure to hear him read them," even though Shelley was no actor, nor even a man known for an excellent speaking voice.[9] I had never heard one of my friends read a single Shakespeare play, nor had I read one out loud myself in its entirety, although I did subject my children to a condensed soup version of *The Tempest* when they were very small and I wanted them to sit through Shakespeare in the park. I was used to being entertained without giving performers my full consideration. The speaker on the radio, the television actor, the movie star—none of them cared whether I was wiping gunk out of a cat's eye while I was listening. Attention did not have to be paid.

Romantic theatergoers, by contrast, were so attentive they noticed the smallest alteration in a particular performance. They were capable of registering not only how Siddons deviated from Mrs. Pritchard, but also how Siddons deviated from her prior self if, for example, she performed while suffering a head cold. When Siddons canceled one of her Edinburgh performances as Constance in *King John* because of being "severely indisposed with a cold and hoarseness," she caused a newspaper reviewer to comment, "Having witnessed, during her performances on the nights on which she ventured to appear, decided symptoms of this harassing complaint, we were glad that she had at length determined to allow herself some respite."[10] The *King John* performance was supposed to take place on Saturday, 17 March. The newspaper reviewer had presumably seen Siddons perform as Lady Macbeth on Wednesday, as Zara in *The Mourning Bride* on Thursday, and, quite possibly, again as Lady Macbeth on Friday. Cultural memory operated in much the same manner as bootleg concert recordings of the Grateful Dead, allowing the Siddons connoisseur to hear her voice speaking a line against an audio backdrop of prior renderings of the same theatrical moment.

In his history of ventriloquism, Steven Connor claims that the "rapid naturalization of the technologically mediated voice" has resulted in a loss of a kind, that is, "the loss of the loss of the voice."[11] We have been severed, Connor goes on to write, "not from our voices but from the pain of that severance" (411). Connor suggests those who listened in advance of sound recording technology experienced a tragic sense of the ephemerality of the voice. Certainly Bell's notes serve to confirm Connor's assertion. Only a man who had a keen awareness of the fleeting nature of Siddons's voice would pencil his way through Siddons's performances, creating his own shorthand to document her voice's tone and emphasis. On the other hand, Bell and his contemporaries had voices more firmly traced on their memories; they sought ways to preserve Siddons's voice mainly so that it wouldn't be lost to future generations. They, themselves, carried Siddons's voice in their heads. By contrast, the ability to record the voice with a machine may have caused people to listen less carefully since the voice could always be replayed. Even as the voice has become ever more easily recordable, transferrable, and portable, it may have slipped farther out of memory's reach.

The loss of the loss of the voice . . . the loss of the loss of the voice. Connor's phrase seemed like the answer to a question I'd never asked. Was I only interested in Siddons's voice because I would never be able to hear it? Was I nostalgic for a moment when people had not suffered the loss of the loss of the voice, but when people were also not suffering the loss of the voice because they had so many voices ringing in their heads? I recalled the once-a-year television screenings of *The Wizard of Oz* that took place before the advent of the VCR, and also the looped screening of the film that a grad school friend used to occupy his daughter while he was cramming for an exam. His four-year-old watched *The Wizard of Oz* six times in a row as he speed-read *The Faerie Queen* and *Middlemarch*. Could Margaret Hamilton's voice, endlessly replayed over a long day, be as thrilling for that four-year-old as it was for me when I was four and had to wait twelve months to hear her melt into a puddle of witch? Did either of us hear, really hear, Hamilton's voice in the same way romantic listeners heard Siddons, that is, with a whole retinue of other actors' voices vying for their attention in memory's recording studio?

One commentator on Bell's notes called them far superior to a phonograph recording. Brander Matthews, in his 1915 introduction to Jenkin's two essays on Siddons, made the surprising claim that Bell's efforts at preservation surpassed the productions of the new recording technology. "In the future," wrote Matthews, "the phonograph may preserve for us the voice of an honored performer; and thus supply material for opinion about the quality of his tones and the justice of his readings." But Matthews continued, "At best, these will be but specimen bricks, and we shall still lack the larger outlines of the performance as a whole." He believed that there was a "phenomenal value" in the record that Jenkin preserved of Bell's experience "while he was actually under the spell of Mrs. Siddons's enchantment."[12] The explanation for Matthews's favoring of Bell's notes over a phonograph recording lies, I believe, in Bell's attempt to convey what it felt like to hear Siddons perform as well as to convey the quality of her voice as she acted in particular scenes. In calling the phonograph recording a specimen brick, Matthews alludes to the story of a man who attempted to show what his house looked like by displaying one brick. The phonograph record, Matthews feared, removed the voice from its several contexts: from the actors' movements, from the reactions of other actors on stage, and from the audience's response. A similar fear suffuses Wordsworth's effort to preserve the voice of a solitary reaper; his poem's many levels of disconnection from the woman's song stoke doubts about the faithfulness and authenticity of the version of the woman's voice that the poem's narrator attempts to carry away.[13]

Through Bell's notes, Brander Matthews claimed, we become "sharers in the pleasure of the performance and appreciators of at least a few of its manifold merits" (20). I had mulled over Bell's observations—first as they were transcribed by Jenkin, then in the original, and finally in a digitized copy of a microfilm of the original—but still I did not know what it felt like to be "under the spell of Mrs. Siddons's enchantment." Even if I could be whisked back to 1809 and take a seat in the Covent Garden theater, even if George Joseph Bell was jabbing me with his elbow or Joseph Severn was hyperventilating by my side, I would not be an equal sharer in the pleasures of Siddons's performances because I would not, like Severn and Bell—like almost anyone who went to the theater in the romantic period—have a vast dramatic repertoire filed away in my brain, with subfiling for variant performances of particular roles. I would sit like a listening-impaired lump, clutching a sad little clothespin bag of Shakespeare quotations, while Siddons made the rest of the audience resonate like harp strings.

Chapter Fourteen

I decided to make one last-ditch effort to become the kind of listener who could appreciate Siddons. Belatedly determined to listen to Siddons's most famous speeches, even if I could only hear them spoken by actors who came after her, I descended into the nether regions of the library's media center. A work study student with a Shuffle clipped to her jeans led me to a listening booth that turned out to be a museum of old recording devices. There was a flat rectangular cassette player of the kind I used to listen to the Jackson Five when I was in the fifth grade. There was a boxy turntable like the one on which my oldest sister played Kingston Trio LPs during the Kennedy administration. There were headphones the size of cinnamon buns.

Through careful listening to a daisy chain of Lady Macbeths, I sought to become more like one of Siddons's original audience members, but I also cherished a secret hope that I would come across some audio vestige of Siddons's performance, passed down from one actress to another, like the Bernhardt handkerchief that got passed down from Helen Hayes to Julie Harris to Cherry Jones.[1] Donning headphones, I began by listening to Fiona Shaw perform Lady Macbeth for the Naxos Audio Book version of *Macbeth* in a CD format. Fiona Shaw was a breathless Lady Macbeth, who read nearly all of her lines as if she has just run up stairs. When she read Macbeth's letter, she laughed a little before she spoke the words "Thane of Cawdor," as if the idea tickled and delighted her. When she delivered Lady Macbeth's most famous line—"Come, you spirits / That tend on mortal thoughts, unsex me here"—she spoke as if she were gasping for air. And when she gave Macbeth his marching orders ("look like the innocent flower, / But be the serpent under't"), she did so with a smile in her voice. The Naxos Audio Book version of *Macbeth* was not subtle in its use of sound effects. The dripping sounds that could be heard throughout the play intensified before Lady Macbeth's hand-washing scene, as if someone had opened a spigot. When Macduff cried "Awake, awake!" after discovering Duncan's murder, an alarm clock rang.

Perhaps because it was an audio rendering, and because I was sitting in an isolation booth with nothing to look at except a digital display, the Naxos Audio Book version brought home to me, in ways that subsequent watchings of *Macbeth* on DVD and VHS would not, that the role of Lady Macbeth encourages virtuoso voice work. In the banquet scene, as Fiona Shaw played it, Lady Macbeth switched back and forth between two voices. She used a low, hale voice when trying to calm the dinner guests, and she adopted a high nervous voice when trying to curb her husband's odd behavior. In the sleepwalking scene, Fiona Shaw had a different voice for every line. She said "Fie, my lord" flirtatiously, "Where is she now?" furiously, and "Wash your hands" urgently. When she spoke the line "I tell you yet again, Banqo's buried," she did so in a furious shriek, but she immediately simmered down enough to say, "come, come, give me your hand," very evenly, as if she were talking to a child.

Subsequent Lady Macbeth recordings did not shake my conviction that the role was made for actresses who could play their voices like musical instruments. When Jane Lapotaire performed the sleepwalking scene for a 1983 BBC production, she said "Hell is murky!" in a tearful voice, and she lapsed into a distraught moan when observing that all the perfumes of Arabia would not sweeten her little hand. She spoke the line "Wash your hands" calmly at first, but delivered "Banquo's buried" in a scream. She spoke "To bed, to bed" as if she were warding off a migraine, eyes squinched and hands flailing beside her ears.

Around the time I was switching from Jane Lapotaire's Lady Macbeth to the Lady Macbeth of Francesca Annis, it occurred to me that I was reenacting the recording sessions of George Joseph Bell, except that I was scratching notes on a legal pad while sitting in an isolation booth, rather than penciling marginalia on a play script while sitting in a theater. Also, George Joseph Bell never watched an actress perform the sleepwalking scene in the nude as Francesca Annis was required to do for Roman Polanski's 1971 film version. Perhaps because the director didn't want to risk an X rating, or perhaps because Annis was reluctantly nude, in Polanski's *The Tragedy of Macbeth*, Lady Macbeth speaks the first few lines of the sleepwalking scene sitting down with her back to the audience, and she speaks the final lines in a catatonic state, while being led (and visually blocked) by the Doctor and Gentlewoman.

I watched Francesca Annis on an old VHS cassette, her performance slightly muted by tape decay. Her vocal performance, all things considered, was not as dynamic as that of Jeanette Nolan, the surprise choice to play Lady Macbeth for Orson Welles's 1948 film version, and the first Lady Macbeth in my lineup to speak with a pronounced Scottish burr. Jeanette Nolan was a radio actress, and she was having to hold her own against a Macbeth who wore a boxy crown and swigged from a horn, so she deployed her voice to full advantage. She spoke "Hell is murky!" in a high childish voice, and "all the perfumes of Arabia" in a whining wail. When she said "look not so pale," she spoke as if bossing a subordinate, and when, in a departure from stage tradition, Macbeth barged into the sleepwalking scene as she was saying "To bed, to bed!" she pushed him away and shrieked.

As the day wore on, I grew more like Siddons's listeners because I began to anticipate the play's best lines, and to suffer the many scenes that included no Lady Macbeth merely so that I could get to the banqueting and sleepwalking. But I also became less like Sarah Siddons's listeners because I started fast-forwarding past Banquo's murder and the Macduff family massacre so that I could hear Lady Macbeth without delay. I knew that if I were really going to trace some Siddonian vocal quirk down through her Lady Macbeth descendants, I would need to hear the nineteenth-century actors who most directly followed in her footsteps, starting with her niece Fanny Kemble. But most of those Lady Macbeths had either preceded recording technology or been neglected by Edison and his cohorts. Still, I wanted to believe that Judi Dench, whose 1976 kerchief-wearing Lady Macbeth was voted the greatest performance by an actress in the history of the Royal Shakespeare Company, was Sarah Siddons's inheritor. She made the sleepwalking scene her own by whimpering throughout and by adding a squeal that swelled into a full-blown Munchean scream. Even watching the pixillated version available on YouTube, you can imagine being knocked flat by Dench's performance, but she's so many generations removed from Siddons it's impossible to trace a direct line of vocal descent.

My media center Lady Macbeths did, however, trace a progression through twentieth-century recording history. I had begun by listening to Fiona Shaw on CD and Jane Lapotaire on DVD, then moved on to Francesca Annis and Jeanette Nolan on VHS cassette. Next in my queue was a 1941 Mercury Acting Company production of *Macbeth;* Fay Bainter's Lady Macbeth had been captured on a 78 rpm record, one of nine sturdy stackable disks that preserve the production as a whole. I leaned in to the record player, but before I had been listening to Bainter for more than a few minutes, the turntable, stressed by the exhausting 78 revolutions per minute, started developing a death rattle, and her voice grew inaudible. Summoned to my cubicle, the student worker took a few desultory jabs at the machine's start button without removing her earbuds. For a few seconds we stood over the silenced turntable as if waiting for someone to speak an elegy. Then she got called to fix a jammed copier, and I was on my own.

It was cold in the media center, and the hour was late. Movie voices drifted over from the DVD player next door, a microfilm reader racketed to a halt, and I knew that my pursuit of Siddons's voice was coming to an end. I staggered out of the listening booth, leaving a few stray Lady Macbeths piled up on a library cart.

I hadn't entirely completed my Siddons research. There were things I'd always meant to do that I'd never gotten around to doing. I'd once imagined myself standing on the stage at Richmond, Yorkshire, in a Georgian theater that was, according to Susan C. Law, a helpful British historian with whom I'd corresponded, completely different from any other theater, and with acoustics that were impossible to understand unless you stood inside. I'd also never experienced firsthand the acoustics of another Georgian theater at Bury St. Edmunds, which I'd learned, on the same good authority, was being restored.

I'd only halfheartedly carried out the detective work that Peter Holland helpfully proposes in his essay on David Garrick's voice. He suggests that one might learn about how actors of Siddons's era sounded by consulting John Walker's *A Critical Pronouncing Dictionary, and Expositor of the English Language* (1791) and Thomas Sheridan's *A General Dictionary of the English Language* (1780), works that have been "extensively investigated by historical phonologists but not by theatre histori-ans."[2] I'd looked up a few words from Lady Macbeth's sleepwalking speech in the *Critical Pronouncing Dictionary*, but discovering that, for Siddons, "damned" was probably a two-syllable word with a voiced "n" ("Out, dam-ned spot") didn't get me much closer to how her specific voice sounded.

Nor had I pursued the family angle that had once seemed to hold some promise. Thomas Campbell maintained that Siddons's mother's voice "had much of the emphasis of her daughter's" (1: 4). Siddons's mother hailed from Warwickshire, and I'd wondered if I could pick up some hint of the mother's intonations by listening to West Midlands voices in the British Library's archive of regional accent and dialect recordings, and if a mash-up of West Midlands vocalizations and those of Siddons's own birthplace of Brecknock, South Wales, would produce some approximation of Siddons's way of speaking. And if Siddons sounded like her mother, might not the voices of Siddons's living de-scendants hold a vestige of Siddons's vocal essence, and wouldn't I be able to hear that Siddonian undertone if, say, I called them on the tele-phone and asked them to quote Lady Macbeth?

I never did though. I Googled Siddons's family tree in a halfhearted way, but I never tracked her lineage farther than a Victorian grand-niece. I wasn't really interested in how Siddons sounded on a telephone line even if I could call up Siddons herself and not some distant relative who might be wondering, and not in a pleasantly surprised way, how I'd gotten her number.

I had wanted to find out how Siddons made Severn want to change his life, or, failing that, how she caused so many people to go into con-niptions when she stepped out on stage, but this meant, of course, and I'd known this all along, that I really had to be there. However, in try-ing to pull answers to these impossible questions out of the well-rum-maged effluvia of theater memoirs, newspaper clippings, Siddons let-ters, and fan marginalia, I'd learned many things I hadn't known when I'd started, and so I was qualified to draw a few semiauthoritative con-clusions. Peter Holland, as he's embarking on his discussion of Gar-rick's voice, cheerfully concedes that his article is doomed to failure, that he's going to find himself arguing over tiny matters, and that it's all going to be hopeless. Nevertheless, he soldiers on, speculating wonder-fully about the need "to develop a vocabulary to record in prose (unlike recording on audio cassette) precisely what an actor has sounded like," and drawing our attention to how our inattention to actors' voices markedly contrasts with the acute aural sensitivity of Garrick's peers.[3] Buoyed by Holland's prescriptions, I paused in my accumulation of Siddons arcana and drew conclusions.

CONCLUSION #1 What audience members heard when they witnessed Sarah Siddons perform was, to a large extent, what made them quiver and burst into sobs, what made them succumb to hysteria and collapse in the aisles, and what led them to conjure her performances in conversation years after the fact and to bore younger theatergoers with their insistence that every later actor was no Siddons. How Sarah Siddons sounded was what made her seem so staggeringly original, even though she was acting in a style that would soon be tornadoed off the stage by Edmund Kean, who darted and gesticulated and emoted with a dynamism that made the Kemble school of actors seem like a troupe of superannuated mimes.

If you accept that premise, every Siddons performance comes to seem like a cordoned-off garden of sonic delight. And even the most promising visual representations of Siddons performances, like, say, Henry Fuseli's kinetic oil painting *Lady Macbeth Seizing the Daggers* (fig. 8), come to seem like distractions that will cause you to forget that you can't hear Sarah Siddons's Lady Macbeth and so, therefore, can't know what made Siddons so great.

If you believe, as I've come to believe, that Siddons's voice and delivery were the sources of her triumph, you will find evidence to support that thesis everywhere. *Especially* in Boaden's account of her *Macbeth* performance, an account that begins by asserting that Siddons's "first novelty was a little suspension of the voice," when she read Macbeth's account of the witches, and spoke the phrase "they made themselves—*air*" (*Memoirs of Mrs. Siddons*, 2: 133). And *particularly* when you read Thomas Campbell's description of Siddons's Queen Katherine performance, in which he praises the "clear and intelligent harmony of unlaboured elocution, which unravels all the intricacies of language, illuminates obscurity, and points and unfolds the precise truth of meaning to every apprehension."[4] Convinced that Siddons's voice was the key to her success, you will breeze past Boaden's excursus on Siddons's "*shroud-like* clothing," which was possibly inspired by Joshua Reynolds, so that you can linger over Boaden's comment on Reynolds listening to Siddons from the orchestra. "She was in truth so strongly articulate," Boaden writes, "that I have no doubt he heard every syllable that *breath* made up, for she hardly allowed the voice any portion of its power" (2: 146).

CONCLUSION #2   Siddons's emergence on the London stage was a paradigm-shifting experience, one of several such ground-shaking experiences the romantic theater provided. Tracy Davis compares Kean's celebrated 1814 performance as Shylock to the Beatles's 1964 performance on the *Ed Sullivan Show*.[5] His "emphasizing [of] intense emotions and marked mood swings," she writes, "won out over the neoclassical restrained style of the Kembles, who had seemed to emphasize showing ideals in statuesque standard poses . . . rather than embodying the emotional explosiveness of human experiences in made-to-order fluid combinations."[6]

Siddons's emergence on the London stage caused fans like Joseph Severn to walk out of the theater with a sense of being born anew, and to take up paintbrush and easel in Siddonian apprenticeship. Davis compares Kean's theatrical impact to the advent of gas lighting, which, within three years of the famous Shylock performance, rendered actors newly three-dimensional with its added footcandles of stage illumination.[7] In Davis's perceptive reading of Coleridge's comment that seeing Kean was like reading Shakespeare by flashes of lightning, Siddons and her brother come to seem like the static backdrop to a Keanian revolution, like the wooden stage flats of a creaky bygone theatrical tradition. But the comparatively static quality of the Kemble style—Hazlitt called her Hermione performance, which he admired, monumental, and he likened the aging Siddons to a cast from the antique—only served to amplify the soul-shattering capacity of Siddons's vocal performances.

What does it take to turn a theater actor into a phenomenon, to lift her from the ranks of other admired performers and make of her a cultural obsession? Thomas Betterton was widely admired, his performances lovingly remembered, but he didn't inspire the audience hysteria of a Siddons. Joseph Roach describes Betterton's performance as Alexander the Great in Nathaniel Lee's *Rival Queens* as a royal effigy fabricated from the memories of earlier actors and also earlier kings. He relied on "a minor actor with a long memory" to speak a line as

Charles Hart had spoken it in order that Betterton could make this prior voicing part of his interpretation. Discussing Betterton, Roach suggests that audiences may come to regard a particular performer as "an eccentric but meticulous curator of cultural memory, a medium for speaking with the dead."[8] Siddons broke with cultural memory, toppling the settled accretion of past interpretations and causing audience members to hear familiar lines in new and disconcerting ways.

CONCLUSION #3   Siddons had this unsettling effect because romantic era listeners were keenly attuned to both the sound and the ephemerality of spoken words. If you are predisposed, as the romantics were, to worrying about lost things, to casting a nostalgic glance backward to the people who existed before you and to accumulating those people's papers, medals, and coins, but also those people's poems and stories, literary artifacts that existed primarily as spoken word performances, you are likely to have a particular sensitivity to the fragility and ephemerality of an actor's voice. And if an actor comes along with a way of speaking lines and screaming that seems entirely unprecedented and unlikely to be replicated by future actors, you are going to be especially vulnerable to her allure. Siddons spoke her lines at a moment when people were nostalgic about the past, and so also nostalgic, in an anticipatory way, about the future's past, that is, the point in time (their own point in time) that would become the focus of future nostalgia.[9] Siddons's voice—unique, irreplaceable, transient—came into being at a moment when people were exceptionally preoccupied with ephemeral objects, and with sound, in particular, that most ephemeral of entities. So Siddons became SIDDONS because her particular talent resided in how she sounded when she spoke lines, and because she happened to perform at a moment when listeners were particularly attuned to both the power and the transience of sound.

As Davis notes, Kean's performances were described with the vocabulary of lighting technologies that were just being invented; his Shylock was electric. Siddons's performances were described, often in retrospect, with the vocabulary of sound recording technology whose advent was still decades away. The longing for aural permanency that Edison claimed to satisfy with the phonograph was a longing that saturates romantic culture more generally, and that links theatrical and poetic realms.

"I hear, I hear, with joy I hear!" Wordsworth writes in "Ode: Intimations of Immortality."[10] But in one of his other great poems, "Lines Composed a Few Miles above Tintern Abbey," a "sounding cataract" haunts the poem's narrator "like a passion."[11] Just so did Siddons's voice haunt her audience members, causing some, like Joseph Severn, to change their lives, but causing many others, in later years, to regretfully replay their memories of how she sounded and to worry about all they had lost.

Chapter Fifteen

In 1817, at the age of sixty-two, Sarah Siddons played Lady Macbeth for the last time and was panned by William Hazlitt, who regretted having to record the progress of her decay. He wrote, "Her voice is somewhat broken since last year; her articulation of some words, particularly where the sibillant consonants occur, is defective; and her delivery of the principal passages is unequal, slow, improgressive, and sometimes inaudible." He faulted Siddons's pauses for being "too long and frequent," and for seeming "inexplicable" to persons at a distance, "where the expression of the eye could not fill up the vacancy." He claimed that in the first soliloquy she "laid a disproportionate emphasis, or gave a louder enunciation to some particular words, while the rest of the sentence subsided in lingering murmurs on the ear, or was buried in the deep bosom of thought." There was no reason, Hazlitt claimed, why Siddons pronounced "*sightless* substances" with "a greater elevation of voice than any other word in the same line." Siddons had lost command of her voice, Hazlitt lamented: "She was no longer the same Lady Macbeth, the same overpowering terrific being that she once was."[1]

The performance of *Henry VIII* that Joseph Severn witnessed took place on 31 May 1816, a year before Hazlitt disparaged her Lady Macbeth, but long after her voice had begun to deteriorate from age. As early as 1811, after seeing Siddons play Mrs. Beverley in *The Gamester*, Henry Crabb Robinson commented that although in most respects her acting was not inferior to her former performances, "her Voice appeared to have lost its brilliancy (like a beautiful face through a veil)" (45). After watching her play Queen Katherine in the same *Henry VIII* performance that Severn attended, Robinson wrote, "Mrs Siddons is not what she was—It was with pain that I perceived the effect of the time in the most accomplished of persons—This was more audible to the ear than visible to the eye—There was occasionally an indistinctness in her enunciation and she laboured her delivery most anxiously as if she feared her power of expression was gone" (71). Severn was astounded and unsettled by a Siddons who, in Robinson's account, was well into vocal decline.[2]

Henry Crabb Robinson's diary entries chronicle this decline in excruciating detail. "Her advancing old age is really a cause of pain to me," he wrote in 1811, just after complaining that Siddons's articulation was "indistinct," her voice "more than usually drawling and funereal," during the first act of Franklin's *Earl of Warwick* (34). But Robinson went on to say, "She is the only actor I ever saw with a conviction that there never was nor ever will be her equal" (35). For the rest of his life, Robinson would wield his aural memory of an earlier more pleasing version of Siddons as a cudgel with which to bash actresses who assumed her roles. "I wished not to see Miss O'Neill first in a character in which I had seen Mrs Siddons for who could bear such a trial?" he wrote in 1813, after seeing O'Neill perform in *Isabella* (59). "Mrs West's performance was but a feeble imitation of Mrs Siddons," he wrote in 1822 after seeing West play Lady Macbeth (100). And when he saw Mrs. Sloman play Lady Macbeth eleven years later, "It was absolutely a pain to listen to the vulgar declamations and look on the disgusting countenance of Mrs Sloman with such recollections as I was full of" (138). When, in 1828, he heard the celebrated opera singer Madame Pasta perform as Medea, he was still fixated on Siddons. He wrote afterward, "What would Mrs Siddons have made of such a scene? I am surprised on reflexion that no one made a Medea for her. It ought to have been her very greatest character for it combines every one of the passions in which she excelled—scorn, pity, revenge, love, all blended together" (125).

Severn only heard Siddons after she had descended into what Robinson experienced as her vocal decline, but he showcased her voice in his memory like a beautiful talisman. Severn listened to Siddons long after she had become fixed in a kind of cultural quicksand, apt preparation for her final static role on a Paddington Green pedestal. By the end of the eighteenth century, Shearer West writes, "Siddons is more and more frequently spoken of as a monolithic character in both private and public life, despite the versatility of her roles. She was not a shape changer but an immobile piece of sculpture, the living embodiment of the tragic muse."[3] In 1811, a reviewer faulted Siddons for her "unbending and freezing dignity."[4] She had become known as "The Siddons," and "was recommended to tourists as one of the obligatory sights of London, like the Abbey or the Tower Lions."[5]

Several years had passed since I'd walked around Siddons's statue at Paddington Green, and the monument now inhabited a world in which it was even harder to imagine what it was like to listen to her speak. All around me, people were listening in new ways, ways that mostly involved ignoring proximate human voices. Soon after I started researching this book, a cell phone went off for the first time in my classroom. The cell phone owner scrambled to shut it off, enacting a small Kabuki drama of regret and mortification. A few years later, another cell phone went off in my classroom, and the student took the call, speaking in a low murmur as I tried to carry on with class discussion. As I recall, it was a discussion of Keats's "Ode to a Nightingale," but of course I would want to remember it that way. In "Ode to a Nightingale," Keats describes the nightingale as a transcendent transmitter, whose voice is conveyed, unaltered, over distance and through time:

> The voice I hear this passing night was heard
>   In ancient days by emperor and clown:
> Perhaps the self-same song that found a path
>   Through the sad heart of Ruth, when, sick for home,
>   She stood in tears amid the alien corn;
>   The same that oft-times hath
>   Charm'd magic casements, opening on the foam
>   Of perilous seas, in faery lands forlorn.[6]

Keats's poem suggests that emperor, clown, Ruth, magic casement—figures belonging to different time periods (as well as different literary genres)—all heard the same bird transmission. If you think of the bird song as a form of mass communication, you could say that Keats, anachronistically, is claiming that the bird's audience members, although separated in time, are united by their common listening experience, in the same way that separate visitors to an Internet site, although spread out in time, are united spatially by their common arrival at one site.[7] But this would assume that each auditor listened in the same way and heard the same bird song.

During all the time I was trying to discover how Sarah Siddons sounded, I kept recalling a cartoon reference to Keats's stanza that I'd once seen pinned to the door of a grad student cubicle. It was a sketch of Ruth standing in a cornfield and holding a cordless phone. The caption, as best I can remember it, read, "Ruth phones home amid the alien corn."[8] The cartoon countered Keats's claim that the bird's song was immortal by insisting that historical circumstances alter the way we hear bird songs (and also alter, by the way, how we read the word "corn"— which, for Keats, referred to grain in general and not to the specific ear-yielding plant that sprang to the cartoonist's mind). If the cartoon was created today, Ruth would be texting on her BlackBerry, oblivious to the bird's song. The nightingale's song (or an exhumed Siddons performance) might be the same, or nearly so—but not its listeners.

Not long ago, the lights went off in my neighborhood. There was a big shuddering bang, the sound of a squirrel being electrocuted, and then the street went dark. When I went over to offer some candles to a college student who'd just moved in across the street, and who, bereft of wide-screen TV, was sitting on her front steps in darkness, she could barely stand to interrupt her phone conversation. It was as if the oddest thing in the world had happened, a live human neighbor stood before her and waited to speak. A few doors down, someone started setting off firecrackers. My daughter searched frantically with a flashlight for her iPod. Only the elderly couple who live behind me sat expectantly on their back stoop, ready to swap blackout stories across the alley.

When Thomas Edison invented the phonograph, his agent in England, George Gouraud, used romantic poetry to advertise the new technology, attributing to the phonograph recording the kind of "natural" sound Wordsworth celebrated in one of his bird poems. Gouraud suggested that Edison cloak his new technology in romantic terms by quoting a line from Wordsworth's "To the Cuckoo."[9] He encouraged Edison to introduce his first transatlantic cylinder with the line, "Shall I call thee bird, or but a wandering voice?" Gouraud wrote, "Nothing could be more appropriate than the words, 'But a wandering voice', and I have registered them in connection with the word 'Phonogram'."[10] The line would help to underscore the fidelity of the recorded sound, its indistinguishability from the voice of its maker. But it also, however inadvertently, highlighted the anxiety evoked by detached voices set free to wander aimlessly through the atmosphere.[11] Even if the recorded voice was an exact replica of the original one, its very detachment created listening possibilities that were entirely different from its first aural context. But now we had come full circle: everyone in my neighborhood who wasn't getting invitations to join the AARP preferred voices that were severed from their speakers' bodies, voices that could be conjured or curtailed at will, voices that didn't come offering candles and expecting you to make small talk with a person you hadn't friended.

Edison's claim to being the father of recorded sound was recently challenged by the discovery in Paris of a ten-second recording of a human voice singing "Au Clair de la Lune." The recording was made in 1860, twenty-nine years after Sarah Siddons's death and seventeen years before Edison recorded the words "Mary had a little lamb" on a sheet of tinfoil.[12] The new earliest recording of the human voice sounded terrible. The woman's voice that was singing sounded suspiciously like Sarah Bernhardt's quavery voice, which made me once again doubt my ability to register the fine nuances of early recorded voices, especially when they were struggling to be heard against the kind of scratchy static that, like a jealous backup singer, challenged the "Lune" crooner. You could only tell she was singing "Au Clair de la Lune" if you recognized the tune. Still, the "Lune" recording, recovered through high-resolution scanning of a "phonautogram" created by a French typesetter, moved the advent of sound recording seventeen years closer to the time when Sarah Siddons's voice might have been recorded.

Charles Babbage called the air we breathe "the never-failing historian of the sentiments we have uttered." According to Babbage, "The pulsations of the air, once set in motion by the human voice, cease not to exist with the sounds to which they gave rise," and he raised the possibility that the motions they impressed on the particles of the atmosphere might be traced back to their source if man enjoyed a larger command over mathematical analysis.[13] The logician Charles Sanders Peirce, born eight years after Siddons's voice passed into its afterlife, predicted that a day would come when we would be able to hear the voices of people who died long before the advent of the phonograph or the phonautogram. "Give science only a hundred more centuries of increase in geometrical progression," he wrote, "and she may be expected to find that the sound waves of Aristotle's voice have somehow recorded themselves."[14] Give science enough time, and she may be expected to find that the soundwaves of Siddons's voice had somehow recorded themselves. Or so we'd like to believe. Trapped in some long-dead prompter's attic, amid yellowing play scripts, they are waiting perhaps to be found.

Romantic theatergoers had Siddons's voice imprinted on their memories. I, too, have voices imprinted on my memory, but mostly they are nontheatrical ones. I can hear in my mind's ear my children's voices, and the voice of my husband. I can conjure the squawk of my neighbor's voice on the speaker phone she started using after she suffered a small stroke. I can call to mind the rumbling sound the dog makes in the middle of the night when the cat finds his collar in the leash basket and pulls it, tags rattling, up the stairs.

Has a stage actor made a profound impression on me? Yes: Marian Seldes performing the role of Woman in Edward Albee's *The Play About the Baby*. If, after I saw Seldes perform in *The Play About the Baby*, the president of her fan club had been soliciting new members in the theater lobby, gladly would I have slapped my dues on his card table, and recited, in my flat nasal voice, the club pledge. But months after the event I recalled little of how Seldes sounded. The only theater actor's voice I have imprinted on my memory is the voice of an itinerant performer in the Iowa City summer Shakespeare circuit, a woman who has played several major roles over the course of three seasons, so that when, one July, I heard Perdita voice her first lines, I could hear the Cordelia and Viola of summers past.

This actress was a perfectly good Perdita, but it was the Siddons role that riveted my attention. A tall majestic woman played Hermione, and I perked up when Paulina drew back the curtain in the statue scene. The Iowa City Hermione made a fine statue. She held her frozen position for several long minutes while Leontes spoke his remorse and Perdita expressed, with a soft Midwestern twang, her newfound joy. I stopped listening to what the other characters were saying, however, because I was intent on watching Hermione stand still. No matter how hard I stared, I couldn't detect the slightest movement of her body parts.

Time passed.

She didn't even blink.

I began to understand what romantic era audiences found magical about this moment on stage. Even though I was sitting in a high school auditorium where I had recently heard the school principal announce his dress code policy at Back to School Night, I almost grasped what it was like to experience Sarah Siddons playing one of her most famous scenes. The actress playing Hermione, like Siddons before her, performed the scene with monumental dignity and noble aplomb, and her fellow cast members telegraphed their complicated emotions without stealing focus. When the statue slowly and dramatically came alive, I could nearly feel the candle wax dripping in the Covent Garden theater.

But then, at Paulina's urging, Hermione began to speak, and I knew it was not Siddons I heard, nor would hear, no matter how carefully I listened.

Notes

PREFACE

1. Anna Seward to Rev. T. S. Whalley, 7 June 1799, in *Letters of Anna Seward,* 5: 240.

CHAPTER ONE

1. The character Irwin makes this comment in Alan Bennett's play *The History Boys* (25). Geoff Dyer makes a similar point in his meditation on World War I memorials. He writes, "Over the years, passing by in a bus or on a bike, I have seen the Cenotaph so often that I scarcely notice it. It has become part of the unheralded architecture of the everyday. The empty tomb has become the invisible tomb" (*Missing of the Somme,* 19).

2. Sharp, *Life and Letters of Joseph Severn,* 11 (hereafter cited in text). Sharp's edition of Severn's letters combines quotes from Severn's letters with Sharp's paraphrasing of them. In subsequent references, I specify which quotes are Sharp's words and which are Severn quotes.

3. Seward, *Swan of Lichfield,* 68.

4. Thomas Erskine, Harvard Theatre Collection, TS 1272 74, p. 32.

5. Boaden, *Memoirs of Mrs. Siddons,* 1: 327 (hereafter cited in text).

6. "Theatrical Farewells. Garrick and Siddons," 164.

7. O'Keefe, *Edwin's Pills to Purge Melancholy,* vi–vii.

8. Gosse, "Sarah Siddons," 382.

9. Asleson, *Notorious Muse.*

10. Highfill, Burnim, and Langhans, *Biographical Dictionary of Actors.* The catalog of Siddons images comes at the end of the Siddons entry in vol. 14.

11. See, e.g., William H. Galperin's *The Return of the Visible in British Romanticism* and Gillen D'Arcy Wood's *The Shock of the Real: Romanticism and Visual Culture, 1760–1860.*

12. According to the painting's skillful exegetes, Shelley Bennett and Mark Leonard, "She holds her upraised hand with a slightly extended index finger, a gesture that suggests that she is about to speak; her slightly parted lips heighten this effect." See Shelley Bennett and Mark Leonard, "'Sublime and Masterly Performance,'" 115–16.

13. I could, however, apprehend many other facets of her performances thanks to the essays gathered by Robyn Asleson in *A Passion for Performance*. See also Backscheider, *Spectacular Politics*; Buchanan, "Sarah Siddons and Her Place in Rhetorical History"; Julie Carlson, *In the Theatre of Romanticism*; Donkin, "Mrs. Siddons Looks Back in Anger"; Engel, "Personating of Queens"; Oya, *Representing Shakespearean Tragedy*; Richards, *Rise of the English Actress*; Roach, *Player's Passion*; Rogers, "'Towering Beyond Her Sex'"; Straub, *Sexual Subjects*; Woo, *Romantic Actors and Bardolatry*.

CHAPTER TWO

1. James, *Aspern Papers*, 8.

2. Silsbee's memorandum notes are among the holdings of the Peabody Essex Museum in Salem, Massachusetts. I quote from passages reprinted in Marion Kingston Stocking's *Clairmont Correspondence*, 2: 657.

3. Medwin, *Life of Percy Bysshe Shelley*, 250; Hogg, "Life of Shelley," 1: 48; Peacock, *Memoirs of Percy Bysshe Shelley*, 55–56. All of these references were brought to my attention by David Perkins's "How the Romantics Recited Poetry," 656–57, 668n.

4. "What would we not give for a gramophone record of Wordsworth reading his poems aloud during the period covered by Dorothy's journal? or of Keats saying his Odes?" writes Francis Berry in *Poetry and the Physical Voice* (194).

5. Qtd. in Perkins, "How the Romantics Recited Poetry," 659.

6. Perkins, "How the Romantics Recited Poetry," 660 (hereafter cited in text).

7. Jones suggests that attention to "the representation of sound in Wordsworth's poetry specifically, and in romanticism generally, can open us up to a wider world without either setting sound against sight or relying on the standard rejection of the material for it to do so" ("Sounds Romantic"). Susan Wolfson's gathering of essays, *"Soundings of Things Done,"* also enriches our understanding of romantic writers' engagement with sound.

8. Macdonald and Scherf, introduction to Polidori, *Vampyre: A Tale and Ernestus Berchtold*, 29.

9. Weiner, "Listening with John Clare," 377.

10. Wolfson, "Sounding Romantic: The Sound of Sound," in *"Soundings of Things Done."* Wolfson's essay drew my attention to Wordsworth's comment, as well as to many other instances of Coleridge's preoccupation with sound.

11. Wordsworth, *Poetical Works*, 3: 77.

12. The "beautiful sentence" passages from Dorothy Wordsworth's *Recollections of a Tour Made in Scotland* and the quote from Wilkinson's *Tours* are provided in a note to the poem (Wordsworth, *Poetical Works*, 3: 444–45). Wilkinson's travel narrative, which Wordsworth read in manuscript, was not published until 1824.

13. Wordsworth, *Poetical Works*, 3: 444.

14. Corbin, *Village Bells*, xii.

15. Picker, *Victorian Soundscapes*, 11.

16. Mark M. Smith, *Listening to Nineteenth-Century America*, 7–8.

17. There are also a growing number of studies focusing on sound in the early modern period. See, e.g., Bruce R. Smith's *Acoustic World of Early Modern England*, Richard Cullen Rath's *How Early America Sounded*, and Gina Bloom's *Voice in Motion*. Emily Thompson, in *The Soundscape of Modernity*, her study of evolving architectural acoustics in early twentieth-century America, points out that a soundscape "is simultaneously a physical environment and a way of perceiving that environment; it is both a world and a culture constructed to make sense of that world" (1).

18. Langan and McLane, "Medium of Romantic Poetry," 244.

19. Also, I wasn't entirely convinced that silent reading became the new norm, an assertion Langan and McLane adopt from Friedrich Kittler (who was writing about Germany), even as they go on to concede and helpfully discuss the ways in which romantic poems moved back and forth between oral and print renditions. It seems clear that people kept burbling poetry to each other even as the printing presses clattered, so Kittler's premise doesn't seem to hold true for England. Peter Manning makes this same point in his rejoinder to Langan's earlier essay "Understanding Media in 1805." Manning responds to Langan's proposition that "the very blankness of verse—that is, the fully residual status of sound—is constitutive of the poetry of print culture" by reminding us that readers use subvocalization—"an important mode midway between oral delivery and silent reading"—as they run their eyes across a line of print. Manning also insists that "the practice of 'singing or saying' verse was widespread, and the romantic poet expected readers to duplicate the practice in their own encounter with the printed text" ("'Birthday of Typography,'" 75, 76). Nevertheless, Langan's "Understanding Media in 1805" provides a boffo reading of *The Lay of the Last Minstrel*, suggesting that Scott's poem makes the medium of print recognizable *as* a medium by drawing our attention to how it delivers audiovisual information.

20. Benjamin, "Work of Art in the Age of Its Technological Reproducibility," 104–5 (hereafter cited in text).

21. Rachel Brownstein describes a similar enshrinement of the French actress Rachel: "In the last three decades of the nineteenth century, while Sarah Bernhardt dominated the theatrical scene, nostalgia moved garrulous old men to recall the wonderful earlier actress who seemed to incarnate their own lost youth" (*Tragic Muse*, 63).

22. In his reading of the poem as the product of a wartime England "divided by momentous questions of foreign policy and by shifts of economic power that disrupted the traditional alignment of the classes," Peter Manning draws our attention to the two-year gap between the Wordsworths' Scots tour and the writing of the poem, a gap that replicates "the uncrossed barrier between the speaker and the girl" ("Will No One Tell Me What She Sings?" 266–67, 255).

23. Crary, *Techniques of the Observer*, 6, 9.

24. Peters, "Helmholtz, Edison, and Sound History," 179 (hereafter cited in text). See also John M. Picker's lucid explanation of Helmholtz's discoveries in *Victorian Soundscapes*, 84–88.

25. Sterne, *Audible Past*, 107 (hereafter cited in text).
26. Kittler, *Gramophone, Film, Typewriter*, 16.
27. Kittler, "Man as a Drunken Town-Musician," 639.

CHAPTER THREE

1. Clipping, 28 June 1897, box 3, folder 6, Sarah Siddons Society Archive, Chicago Public Library.
2. Qtd. in Kilgarriff, "Henry Irving and the Phonograph."
3. *A Catalogue of the Excellent Household Furniture, a Small Library of Books, Paintings, Wines and Sundry Effects, Late the Genuine Property of Mrs. Siddons*, 4–7.
4. Edison, "Phonograph and Its Future," 534.
5. Edison, *Diary and Sundry Observations*, 83.
6. Kilgarriff, "Henry Irving and the Phonograph."
7. Kilgarriff, "Henry Irving and the Phonograph."
8. Koestenbaum, *Queen's Throat*, 83.
9. Qtd. in Donaldson, *Actor-Managers*, 47.
10. Kilgarriff, "Henry Irving and the Phonograph."
11. Hatton, "Irving Reminiscence," 136. See John Picker's excellent discussion of this episode in *Victorian Soundscapes* (119).
12. Ockman and Silver, *Sarah Bernhardt*. Ockman and Silver's anthology is the exhibition catalog for the Bernhardt exhibition they co-curated at the Jewish Museum (New York).
13. Strachey was describing Bernhardt's delivery of a line from Racine's *Phédre*. Strachey, "Sarah Bernhardt," 470. My attention was drawn to this, and the next several references to Bernhardt's voice, by Karen Levitov's "The Divine Sarah and the Infernal Sally."
14. Sigmund Freud to Martha Bernays, 8 Nov. 1885, in *Letters of Sigmund Freud*, 180.
15. Qtd. in Abdy, "Sarah Bernhardt and Lalique," 325.
16. Feinstein, "Sarah Bernhardt and the Bettini Recording Legacy."
17. "Phonograph and Its Improvements," 82–83.
18. Menefee, *Sarah Bernhardt in the Theatre of Films and Sound Recordings*, 41.
19. Ashton, *Pictures in the Garrick Club*, xxv. Joseph Donohue notes, too, that in the early days of commercial photography, theatrical photographers used stock backgrounds when photographing characters in scenes from plays. Donohue writes, "A scholar unaware of this fact who thought that the photographs were taken on the stage could misinterpret these background scenes as representing the actual scenery of the play, with catastrophic effects on the analysis of the mise-en-scène" ("Evidence and Documentation," 193–94).
20. Ockman, "Was She Magnificent?" 25.
21. Clipping, 28 June 1897, box 3, folder 6, Sarah Siddons Society Archive, Chicago Public Library. One of those performers may have been the British actress Sybil Thorndike (1882–1976), who would also come to take an interest in the statue, presiding in 1952 over a celebration to mark its renovation. By that year, the

Siddons statue had lost part of its nose, several fingers, and its left foot to vandals, and Siddons's descendants had intervened to have it repaired. Thorndike's "informal and charming address" culminated a "pious pilgrimage" that had begun at the statue, gone on to the grave, and ended at Paddington Chapel (Clipping, 26 September 1952, box 3, folder 6, Sarah Siddons Society Archive, Chicago Public Library). Thorndike, like Irving, was an aging actor when she presided over the ceremony; four years later she would give her farewell performance in *Arsenic and Old Lace*. And Thorndike had her voice recorded, so that, by means of the *Great Historical Shakespeare Recordings* compilation, I can hear her play Lady Macbeth with a clipped Scottish accent.

CHAPTER FOUR

1. Campbell, *Life of Mrs. Siddons*, 1: 17 (hereafter cited in text).

2. Qtd. in Manvell, *Sarah Siddons*, 23. Siddons had apparently already had an interview with Garrick years earlier, at which time she had solicited his judgment and protection. According to James Boaden, she impressed Garrick with her recitation of some of the speeches from Nicholas Rowe's *The Tragedy of Jane Shore*. Boaden writes, "Mr. Garrick seemed highly pleased with her utterance and her deportment; wondered how she had got rid of the old song, the provincial Ti-tum-ti; told her how his engagements stood with the established heroines Yates and Younge, admitted her merits, regretted that he could do nothing for her— and wished her—a good morning" (Boaden, *Memoirs of Mrs. Siddons*, 1: 22). By "Ti-tum-ti," Garrick seems to be referring to a singsong quality in the conventional oratory style of the provincial actor.

3. Royde-Smith, *Private Life of Mrs. Siddons*, 40, 37.

4. Downer, "Players and Painted Stage: Nineteenth Century Acting," 522. Downer wrote a two-part analysis of eighteenth- and nineteenth-century acting styles. The first part, "Nature to Advantage Dressed: Eighteenth-Century Acting," was published in *PMLA* in 1943. "It is not to be denied that the great mass of late eighteenth century plays make today but dull reading," writes Allardyce Nicoll in *A History of English Drama* (3: 1).

5. *The Earl of Warwick* was Thomas Franklin's 1792 translation of Jean-François de La Harpe's 1763 tragedy *Warwick*.

6. Phelan, *Unmarked*, 31.

7. Kennedy, "Confessions of an Encyclopedist," 33.

8. Bratton, *New Readings in Theatre History*, 7.

9. Roach, introduction to "Theater History and Historiography," 293. To get a sense of the variety of ways in which critical theory has come to inform the study of performance, see *The Cambridge Companion to Performance Studies*, ed. Tracy C. Davis, and *The Routledge Reader in Politics and Performance*, ed. Lizbeth Goodman and Jane de Gay. For a clear statement of theater history's methodological paradigm shift, followed by an analysis of how the field might benefit from a scholarly exchange with cultural anthropology, see Balme, "Cultural Anthropology and Theatre Historiography," 33–52.

10. Postlewait and McConachie, introduction to *Interpreting the Theatrical Past*, ix, xi.

11. Vince, "Theatre History," 12 (hereafter cited in text). See also Robert D. Hume's essay on the aims, materials, and methodology of theater history. It begins, "'Theatre history' is a discipline much practised but severely under-theorized." Hume goes on to say, "We now work in a postpositivist world and we cannot simply assume that cheery antiquarianism is a thing good in itself" ("Theatre History, 1660–1800," 9).

12. Sarlós, "Performance Reconstruction," 199 (hereafter cited in text).

13. And not just the contributors to this volume. Peter Holland, in Worthen and Holland, *Theorizing Practice*, comments on "a crucial and often disabling tendency in theater history to provide nothing more than a chronological non-analytic history" (16). Janelle G. Reinelt, in her introduction to "Semiotics and Deconstruction," writes, "The logos of 'fact' has legitimated and enforced traditional scholarship and interpretation," before positing a "'fresh' interpretation" that would require "destabilizing the taken-for-grantedness of the production of meaning." See Reinelt and Roach, *Critical Theory and Performance*, 113. And Joseph Roach notes the way in which the history of theater "has struggled with its own oedipal ambivalence toward positivism." See Roach, introduction to "Theater History and Historiography," 293.

14. Case, "Theory/History/Revolution," 427 (hereafter cited in text).

15. Phelan, *Unmarked*, 146. Still, Phelan underscores the presentness of the theatrical past in her reading of Tom Stoppard's *Hapgood* "in terms of the phantom which haunts the theatrical past, the previous performance" (29), as well as in her discussion of how the artist Sophie Calle replaced missing paintings with people's memories of them. Phelan writes, "By placing memories in the place of paintings, Calle asks that the ghosts of memory be seen as equivalent to 'the permanent collection' of 'great works'" (147).

16. Roach, *Cities of the Dead*, 3. Roach claims that the actor's body is itself a museum of past theater performances. "Even in death actors' roles tend to stay with them," Roach writes. "They gather in the memory of audiences, like ghosts, as each new interpretation of a role sustains or upsets expectations derived from the previous ones" (*Cities of the Dead*, 78).

17. Marvin Carlson, *Haunted Stage*, 11.

18. Marvin Carlson, *Haunted Stage*, 13.

19. Marvin Carlson, *Haunted Stage*, 65.

20. Bratton, Bush-Bailey, and DT2323AS Semester 97/8B, "Management of Laughter," 186. "Critical and scholarly discourse about the writings of 1817—Modernist disdain of melodrama, the developing discourses of British Romanticism, and new insights into the Gothic—suggest one set of contexts" for the play, Bratton maintains, but she goes on to say that these contexts were radically challenged by the more physical classroom experiment. Bratton advocates a kind of postmodern reenactment exercise, antiquarianism merged with modern contexts. "The pedagogic engagement of the play with modern film (with Sigourney Weaver and James Whale's *Frankenstein*) and with techniques such as mask work offered

more access than could the library to the spectacle and excitement of *Camilla*," Bratton writes (203).

21. Roach, *Cities of the Dead*, 82.

22. Susan Leigh Foster writes that the kinesthetic sense "has been largely ignored in theories of performance," even though, at least for those in dance studies, "it remains a predominant aspect of aesthetic experience." She goes on to suggest that when we watch a performance, our kinesthetic experience "is contingent, in part, on the conception of the body that pervades our historical moment" ("Movement's Contagion," 46, 57). Baz Kershaw writes about the immersive somatic experience provided by pounding on the engine of a rotting ship, the SS *Great Britain*. He writes, "Some truths concerning the past were resuscitated in the present through knowledge created *in* performance. The feedback of excessive vibration resulted in the collective practices of popular historiography that even now may be helping keep the dead hulk 'alive'" (Kershaw, "Performance as Research," 36).

CHAPTER FIVE

1. Alden Whitman's obituary of Cornell quotes the *New York Times* drama critic Brooks Atkinson: "By the crescendo of her playing, by the wild sensitivity that lurks behind her ardent gestures and her piercing stares across the footlights she charges the drama with a meaning beyond the facts it records." See Alden Whitman, "Katharine Cornell is Dead at 81," *New York Times*, 10 June 1974, http://www.nytimes.com/learning/general/onthisday/bday/0216.html?scp=1&sq= Katharine%20Cornell%20Dead&st=cse (accessed 1 Apr. 2010). A glimpse of Cornell's Juliet performances survives in the 1943 film *Stage Door Canteen*.

2. Leigh-Johnson, "Voice for Actors."

3. "Theatrical Intelligence," *Morning Post*, 1 Jan. 1776.

4. "Theatrical Intelligence," *Morning Post*, 2 Jan. 1776.

5. "Theatrical Intelligence," *Morning Post*, 16 Jan. 1776.

6. William Enfield's chief contributions to improving the speaking habits of the British populace bookended Siddons's emergence on the London stage. His collection of extracts for practicing the art of elocution, *The Speaker*, was published in 1774; the supplemental *Exercises in Elocution* appeared in 1780.

7. Sheridan, *Course of Lectures on Elocution*, 114 (hereafter cited in text). See also Andrew Elfenbein's insights into the way in which "elocution became a technology of transmission, an interface for translating one medium (print) into another (voice) for the benefit of an audience" (*Romanticism and the Rise of English*, 113).

8. Belton, *Random Recollections of an Old Actor*, 206.

9. McKellen, foreword, xii.

10. Rodenburg, *Right to Speak*, 19.

11. *Morning Chronicle*, 30 Dec. 1775.

12. Quoted in Stone, *London Stage*, part 4, 1747–1776, 1941.

13. *Morning Post*, 30 Dec. 1775.

CHAPTER SIX

1. Barthes, "Grain of the Voice," 276 and 270 (hereafter cited in text).

2. As Mladen Dolar writes, "We can almost unfailingly identify a person by the voice, the particular individual timbre, resonance, pitch, cadence, melody, the peculiar way of pronouncing certain sounds. The voice is like a fingerprint, instantly recognizable and identifiable" (*Voice and Nothing More*, 22).

3. Dunsby, "Roland Barthes and the Grain of Panzéra's Voice," 118 (hereafter cited in text).

4. Sharp, *Life and Letters of Joseph Severn*, 14n.

5. Rachel Brownstein suggests that the French actress Rachel, who also dazzled audiences, used her voice to merge with audience members. She writes, "Submitting to her audience's gaze while her voice took their minds over, she destabilized the opposition of self and other—and male and female, subject and object, creator and creation, High and Low" (*Tragic Muse*, 44).

6. Burnim, *David Garrick, Director*, 16–17.

7. Siddons, *Reminiscences*, 5 (hereafter cited in text).

8. Dolar, *Voice and Nothing More*, 14 (hereafter cited in text).

9. Quoted in Siddons entry, in Highfill, Burnim, and Langhans, *Biographical Dictionary of Actors*, 14: 8.

10. Horace Walpole to Lady Ossory, 3 Nov. 1782, in *Horace Walpole's Correspondence with the Countess of Upper Ossory*, 2: 359.

11. Quoted in Manvell, *Sarah Siddons*, 71.

12. Shaughnessy, "Sarah Siddons."

13. Belton, *Random Recollections of an Old Actor*, 151.

14. Boucicault, *Art of Acting*, 29. See also James Murdoch's recollections of this mode of speaking. Murdoch, *The Stage*, 48–49.

15. Barthes, "Phantoms of the Opera," 184 (hereafter cited in text as "Phantoms").

16. Holland, "Hearing the Dead," 249.

17. Wood, "How Shakespeare's 'Irresponsibility' Saved Coleridge," 51–52.

18. Wood, "How Shakespeare's 'Irresponsibility' Saved Coleridge," 46.

CHAPTER SEVEN

1. Coleridge, *Collected Works*, 16: 164 (hereafter cited in text).

2. In an elegant account of the poem's circle of influence, Peter Manning writes, "Coleridge, withholding 'Christabel' from publication between 1797 and 1816, enables it to make its underground reputation through rhapsodes such as [John] Stoddart," whose recitation of the poem informed Sir Walter's Scott's *The Lay of the Last Minstrel*, and, at second hand (through Scott's subsequent recitation), Byron's *The Siege of Corinth* ("'Birthday of Typography,'" 82–83).

3. William Hazlitt, review of "Christabel," 531.

4. Polidori, *Diary*, 128.

5. Byron, *Letters and Journals*, 4: 319.

6. Holmes, *Shelley*, 345.

7. Lamb, "On the Tragedies of Shakspeare," 99 (hereafter cited in text). Lamb, by his own account, had no ear for singing voices, which may help explain his preference for reading, rather than listening to, plays. He professed an inability to distinguish a soprano from a tenor, going on to write, "Only sometimes the thorough bass I contrive to guess at, from its being supereminently harsh and disagreeable" ("Chapter on Ears," 39).

8. The triad, as John Durham Peters describes it, can take the form of message, channel, and senders or receivers, (in the language of information theory) or of programs, institutions and technologies, and audiences (in the field of media studies). Peters, "Mass Media," 267 (hereafter cited in text).

9. McLuhan, *Understanding Media*, 24. For Friedrich Kittler, human beings serve as adjuncts, rather than owners or authors, of media systems. Kittler writes, "The technical differentiation of optics, acoustics, and writing around 1880, as it exploded Gutenberg's storage monopoly, made the fabrication of so-called man possible" (*Literature, Media, Information Systems*, 46).

10. See Barish, *Antitheatrical Prejudice*.

11. The eighteenth-century entertainment venue of the spouting club gave amateur thespians the opportunity to shed the workaday trappings of their normal occupations and don the voices and gestures of celebrity actors. In Thomas Holcroft's 1780 novel, *Alwyn; or, The Gentlemen Comedian*, a lowly clerk performs the dagger scene from *Macbeth* dressed in a habit "made in imitation of Garrick's" (22).

The Spouter's Companion; or, Theatrical Remembrancer was one of many manuals that helped amateur thespians prepare for their moment on stage. It reprints a collection of prologues and epilogues spoken "By the most celebrated Performers of both Sexes," set pieces like the "Prologue to Britannia, A Masque, Spoken by Mr. Garrick, In the Character of a Sailor, fuddled, and talking to himself." Leah Price points out how particular passages of John Home's *Douglas* lived on in recitation manuals long after the play had fallen out of the standard repertoire (*Anthology and the Rise of the Novel*, 79–80).

12. Medwin, *Journal of the Conversations of Lord Byron*, 139. Medwin quotes Byron saying, "Mrs. Siddons was the *beau idéal* of acting; Miss O'Neil I would not go to see, for fear of weakening the impression made by the queen of tragedians. When I read Lady Macbeth's part, I have Mrs. Siddons before me, and imagination even supplies her voice, whose tones were superhuman, and power over the heart supernatural" (138–39).

13. Quoted in J. Fitzgerald Molloy's introduction to *Memoirs of Mary Robinson* (xiv).

14. The proper Siddons inspires less affection than her more profligate rival Dorothy Jordan, who was as renowned in comedy as Siddons was in tragedy. Jonathan Bate links Siddons to the rise of a "defensive middle-class Shakespeare" that resulted from favoring the tragedies over the comedies or romances, *Macbeth* over *Twelfth Night*. Bate concedes, "My argument here has been somewhat pro-Jordan and thus implicitly anti-Siddons," and then goes on to restore a balance by acknowledging the difficulty "of 'reading' the theatre of the era before the advent of audio and video" ("Shakespeare and the Rival Muses," 100–101).

15. Lamb and Lamb, *Tales from Shakespeare*, 2 (hereafter cited in text).
16. Shakespeare, *Macbeth*, ed. Nicholas Brooke, I.vii.54-59.

CHAPTER EIGHT

1. Denby, "Big Pictures," 54.
2. Fitzgerald, *Kembles*, 1: 310.
3. Scott, *Essay on the Drama*, 466 (hereafter cited in text).
4. Peake, *Memoirs of the Colman Family*, 2: 19-20. Colman's comments were brought to my attention by Charles Beecher Hogan's excellent introduction to *The London Stage 1660–1800*, part 5, 1776–1800.
5. Baillie, "To the Reader," xvi (hereafter cited in text).
6. Hazlitt, "Mrs. Siddons," 409.
7. He goes on to distinguish between phonics, or, "the doctrine of sounds," and acoustics, or, "the doctrine of hearing," a distinction Barry Blesser and Linda-Ruth Salter also uphold when they define acoustics as the behavior of soundwaves, and note that "listening is not required." Blesser and Salter use "aural" to refer to the human experience of a sonic process (*Spaces Speak*, 4–5). See Saunders, *Treatise on Theatres*, x and 2 (hereafter cited in text).
8. I have changed "it's" to "its" throughout Saunders's quotes.
9. This was the innovation of the scenographer Phillipe de Loutherbourg, who also projected colored light through transparent scenery in order to realistically simulate different times of day. As scenery and special effects became ever more grandiose and dazzling, actors were in greater danger of being upstaged by their sets.
10. Blesser and Salter, *Spaces Speak*, 2.
11. Thompson, *Soundscape of Modernity*, 205.
12. Bancroft, *Mr. and Mrs. Bancroft On and Off the Stage*, 148.
13. Sandra Richards claims that a theatrical vogue for audience members to shriek along with the heroine originated with Siddons (*Rise of the English Actress*, 79). Play-going was, for romantic viewers, a dialogic experience. Even if they weren't literally responding to the actors on stage—and sometimes they were—audience members talked back to famous performers by speaking familiar lines in their heads and by mimicking them in spouting clubs or in private theatricals. Modern forms of entertainment media—for example, the radio—would seek to re-create the intimacy of live performance. As John Peters writes, "In such techniques as crooning, direct address of listeners, dramatic dialogue, 'feuds' between stars, fan letters, fan clubs, contests and promotional giveaways, or radio comedy, the remote audience was invited to become an imaginary participant in the world of the characters and of its fellow auditors" (*Speaking into the Air*, 216).
14. Haslewood, *Secret History of the Green Rooms*, 1: 14–16. See also Marc Baer's analysis of theater disorder: "Pit, boxes, and galleries became stages themselves, with perorations, dances, mock battles, and demonstrations" (*Theatre and Disorder in Late Georgian London*, 33–34).
15. Hazlitt, *View of the English Stage*, 183.

16. Thompson, *Soundscape of Modernity*, 172.
17. Hazlitt, "Mrs. Siddons," 409.
18. Hazlitt, "Mrs. Siddons," 409.
19. "Well painted passion" is a quote from *Othello*, Act IV, sc. 1. Inchbald, "Remarks," 4.
20. Haslewood, *Secret History of the Green Rooms*, 1: 7–8.

CHAPTER NINE

1. Hunter, "Sleeping Beauties," 3.
2. Wordsworth, Preface to *Poems* (1815), *William Wordsworth*, 632.
3. Wordsworth, Preface to *Poems* (1815), *William Wordsworth*, 632.
4. Hazlitt, *View of the English Stage*, 198.
5. Grover-Friedlander, *Vocal Apparitions*, 3. Michel Poizat suggests these moments are what distinguishes opera from theater: "In opera, the voice does not express the text—that is what theatre is for; the text expresses the voice" (*Angel's Cry*, 145).
6. Dench is quoted in Alastair Macaulay's engrossing discussion of Edith Evans's vocal accomplishments, which is also the source of my description of the handbag line. Macaulay's characterization of Evans's line reading is so good that you may be a little disappointed when you listen to Evans speak the line in the 1951 film version of *Earnest*. He writes, "It has been misdescribed as a crescendo, but at least that draws our attention to something the imitators often overlook: what Evans does with '-bag', starting it with a terrific chest punch and then adding a massive sudden tremolo as the voice continues to ascend" ("Laughter beyond Bracknell," 18).
7. Siddons entry, in Highfill, Burnim, and Langhans, *Biographical Dictionary of Actors*, 14: 20.
8. *Observations on Mrs. Siddons in the Following Characters*, 2 (hereafter cited in text).
9. Aileen Ribeiro notes that when Siddons played Belvidera, she sometimes wore an ultrafashionable French gray satin dress trimmed with dark green, a white satin skirt, and a green hat edged in gold and embellished with ribbons, bows, gauze and feather—a frivolous get-up for the tragic *Venice Preserved*, and one that forces me to see Belvidera's scream in a different light (Ribeiro, "Costuming the Part," 122).
10. Byron was an exception. He wrote to John Murray in Apr. 1827: "I am aware of what you say of Otway—and am a very great admirer of his—all except of that maudlin bitch of chaste lewdness & blubbering curiosity Belvidera—whom I utterly despise, abhor, & detest" (Byron, *Letters and Journals*, 5: 203).
11. Harvard Theatre Collection, TS 1272 74, p. 36.
12. *Modern Stage Exemplified*, 12.
13. Belton, *Random Recollections of an Old Actor*, 29.
14. Pakenham, *Cheltenham*, 63.
15. Staël, *Corinne*, 495 (hereafter cited in text).

CHAPTER TEN

1. Hogan, introduction, lxxxvi. In Leah Wells's memoirs, she reprints some of her positive reviews, such as the one she received from the *Universal Register,* which praised her for introducing "an imitation of Mrs. Siddons, which had a wonderfully fine effect, and was loudly encored by the house." See *Memoirs of the Life of Mrs. Sumbel,* vol. 3, in *Women's Theatrical Memoirs,* ed. Sue McPherson and Julia Swindells, 10: 11.

2. Orgel, introduction to Shakespeare, *Winter's Tale,* 63. See David Worrall's discussion of Queen Caroline's use of this scene as a means of creating sympathy for herself by portraying another beleaguered queen (*Theatric Revolution,* 196–98).

3. Belton, *Random Recollections of an Old Actor,* 90 (hereafter cited in text).

4. Hazlitt, "Winter's Tale," 325.

5. Boaden, *Memoirs of the Life of John Philip Kemble,* 2: 314.

6. Boaden, *Memoirs of the Life of John Philip Kemble,* 2: 314.

7. As Christopher Rovee notes, Hermione is transformed into an aesthetic representation and likened to a portrait miniature long before the statue scene; Leontes complains of Polixenes that he "wears her like a medal, hanging / About his neck," a line that is echoed by Camillo, at the end of the play, when he says of the restored queen, "She hangs about his neck." See Rovee, " 'Everybody's Shakespeare,' " 524–25.

8. Austin, *Chironomia,* 274 and 287 (hereafter cited in text). Austin, an Anglican clergyman, might seem an unlikely person to take up the challenge of finding a way to preserve dramatic performances into perpetuity, but preachers and actors were often yoked in discussions of elocution; their separate attempts to move audiences through vocal intonation and gesture were viewed as common endeavors.

Austin does not have his own entry in the *Dictionary of National Biography,* but he makes a fleeting appearance in the entry devoted to the doomed Irish poet Thomas Dermody, who issued the poetic declaration "I am vicious because I like it," and who published a volume of poems at the expense of the Reverend Gilbert Austin. Austin was likely one of the patrons who gave up on Dermody when he pawned his clothes to keep himself in drink, but his willingness to champion a wayward poet, at least up to a point, suggests both Austin's enthusiasm for art and his counterbalancing standard of decorum. See Jason Edwards's lively account of Dermody in the *Oxford Dictionary of National Biography.*

9. Boucicault, *Art of Acting,* 33.

10. Frances Anne Kemble, *Record of a Girlhood,* 1: 68.

11. Hazlitt, "Miss O'Neill's Juliet," 198.

12. Burwick, "Ideal Shatters," 130.

13. See also Henry Siddons's 1807 *Practical Illustrations of Rhetorical Gesture and Action,* Siddons's son's corrective to Austin's *Chironomia,* and also Lindal Buchanan's discussion of both of these works in "Sarah Siddons and Her Place in Rhetorical History."

14. *Times,* 26 Mar. 1802, qtd. in Bartholomeusz, *Winter's Tale in Performance,* 51.

15. *Morning Chronicle,* 12 Nov. 1807, qtd. in Bartholomeusz, *Winter's Tale in Performance,* 51.

16. *Antigallican Monitor* (1811), 363, qtd. in Bartholomeusz, Winter's Tale *in Performance*, 61.

17. Whitley, *Gainsborough*, 370.

18. *Bell's Weekly Messenger*, 28 Mar. 1802, qtd. in Bartholomeusz, Winter's Tale *in Performance*, 51.

19. "Theatrical Farewells. Garrick and Siddons," 164.

20. Siddons was drawing on a vocabulary of gestures that both predated her acting career and long outlived it, surviving in the histrionic acting style of the early cinema. Roberta Pearson, examining acting styles in American cinema between 1908 and 1913, points back to the nineteenth-century theater tradition of actors playing to the gallery, adhering to a "histrionic code," a gestural communication system that was digital rather than analogic: "Actors deliberately struck attitudes, holding each gesture and abstracting it from the flow of motion until the audience had 'read it'" (*Eloquent Gestures*, 25).

Holding the body in a certain pose spoke "sorrow" or "indignation" or "remorse." But these poses also spoke another phrase: "admire me." The term "claptrap" was originally used to designate those moments when an actor paused long enough to allow an audience to express its admiration with a torrent of applause. An acting style based on silent but expressive pauses also served in the face of less idolatrous audience response. In 1809, protesting changes to the ticket-pricing structure at Covent Garden theater, audiences drowned out the actors with "rattles, bells, cheers, horns, pigs, pigeons, trumpets," thus, "reducing the entire performance to a mime" (Gaull, "Romantic Theater," 256).

21. *The Winter's Tale*, in John Philip Kemble, *Promptbooks*, 9: 78.

22. Shakespeare, *Macbeth*, ed. Nicholas Brooke, I.v.37–42.

CHAPTER ELEVEN

1. One of these was the child actor Master Betty, about whom Siddons's companion Patty Wilkinson expressed reservations. "All that I know of *Master Betty* as you call him, is that he has electrified all the People at Edinbro, Dublin, Birmingham; and in short every place that he has shown his little person in—(he must be an astonishing Child) but that he can be a true portrait of Richard the 3d, Macbeth, Hamlet, &c—*is quite impossible*." See "Letter to Mrs. Piozzi," [5 Oct. 1804], in "The Letters of Sarah and William Siddons to Hester Lynch Piozzi in the John Rylands Library," ed. Kalman A. Burnim, *Bulletin of the John Rylands Library* 52 (Autumn 1969): 77. Henry Crabb Robinson was particularly scathing on Master Betty: "His voice I heard and I never heard a worse. . . . He gave me no pleasure except in the management of his bad voice in scenes of tenderness and gentleness" (*London Theatre*, 48 [hereafter cited in text]).

2. Charles Shattuck's introduction to *Hamlet*, in his edition of Kemble's promptbooks, provides a revealing survey of Kemble's innovations (John Philip Kemble, *Promptbooks*, 2: [i]). Shattuck draws on Boaden's chapter on Kemble's *Hamlet* in *Memoirs of the Life of John Philip Kemble* (1: 88–113).

3. Boaden, *Memoirs of the Life of John Philip Kemble*, 1: 90.

4. Taylor, *Records of My Life*, 270.

5. Hannah Pritchard, in an economical approach to line memorization, focused on her own part to the exclusion of all others. In *Reminiscences*, Siddons recalls discussing her rival with Dr. Johnson. "Is it possible, thought I," Mrs. Siddons writes, "that Mrs. Pritchard, the greatest of all the Lady Macbeths, should never have read the Play? I concluded that he must have been misinformed, but I was afterwards told by a gentleman, an acquaintance of Mrs. P., that he had sup[p]ed with her one night after acting that Part and that he then heard her say she never had read that Play. I cannot believe it" (14).

6. Boaden, *Memoirs of the Life of John Philip Kemble*, 1: 110–11.

7. Boaden, *Memoirs of the Life of John Philip Kemble*, 1: 91–92 (hereafter cited in text as *Kemble*).

8. *Morning Chronicle*, 1 Oct. 1783.

9. Radcliffe, "On the Supernatural in Poetry," 147 (hereafter cited in text). I am grateful to Emily Zaentz for drawing my attention to this Siddons sighting.

10. See Celestine Woo's excellent discussion of this performance in *Romantic Actors and Bardolatry* (117–21), as well as Woo's account of Siddons's Hamlet performance history in "Sarah Siddons as Hamlet."

11. Shaughnessy, "Sarah Siddons." We can perhaps attribute Siddons's Hamlet hiatus to an unwillingness to upstage her brother John Philip Kemble, who debuted in that role at Drury Lane theater in 1783. Siddons played Ophelia to her brother's Hamlet, reportedly in a manner that allowed for a "sensible discrimination, as there ought to be, [of] the real madness of Ophelia from the feigned distraction of Hamlet" (*Public Advertiser*, 17 May 1786, qtd. in Siddons entry, in Highfill, Burnim, and Langhans, *Biographical Dictionary of Actors*, 14: 17).

12. Siddons entry, in Highfill, Burnim, and Langhans, *Biographical Dictionary of Actors*, 14: 16.

13. See Tony Howard's account of Charke's Hamlet in *Women as Hamlet* (36–38).

14. Review in *Monthly Mirror*, May 1796, qtd. in Jane Powell entry, in Highfill, Burnim, and Langhans, *Biographical Dictionary of Actors*, 12: 146.

15. See Robert Shaughnessy's account of this episode in "Sarah Siddons."

16. Galindo, *Mrs. Galindo's Letter to Mrs. Siddons*, 8–10 (hereafter cited in text).

17. Ockman, "Was She Magnificent?" 41.

18. Jenkin, *Mrs. Siddons as Lady Macbeth and as Queen Katharine*, 50.

CHAPTER TWELVE

1. Haydon, *Diary*, 2: 310 (hereafter cited in text).

2. Manning, "Manufacturing the Romantic Image," 228.

3. Claudia Nimbus (Randall McLeod) credits Henderson with being the pioneer of this genre, and in so doing, cites Joseph Chamberlain Furnas's *Fanny Kemble, Leading Lady of the Nineteenth-Century Stage: A Biography* (New York: Dial Press, c. 1982), 322. See Nimbus, "Evening without Mrs Siddons."

4. For an engaging overview of Victorian readers-aloud, see Philip Collins's *Reading Aloud*.

5. The Dublin Lying-in Hospital, although progressive in its approach to ma-

ternity care, must have been a mournful place at the time Siddons was giving her reading. An abstract of the hospital registry provides a statistical glimpse of the women who came through its doors, many of them failing to exit. Between 1797 and 1818, 525 children died in the hospital, and 3,097 infants were stillborn. One in every 100 women who entered the hospital during that period died there, but since not every woman admitted was there to give birth, the death rate for pregnant women was probably much higher, elevated by the epidemic of puerperal fever, known as childbed fever because it was caused by genital-tract sepsis or mastitis ("Abstract of the Registry Kept at the Lying-in Hospital in Dublin"). The Dublin Lying-in Hospital would become one of the first maternity hospitals to insist that doctors wash their hands between deliveries, and to use chloroform for forceps deliveries, and to treat postpartum hemorrhaging, but at the time Siddons was reading Milton, women were giving birth without the benefit of hygiene or painkillers or blood transfusions. See "The History of the Rotunda Hospital." http://www.ie/ library/pdf/rh_hist3.pdf.

6. Mrs. Siddons's Manuscript Copy of Milton's *Paradise Lost*, Houghton 14486.42.5, Houghton Library, Harvard University.

7. Years after the Dublin reading, she would publish a similar abridgement of *Paradise Lost* aimed at children, whose minds, she believed, "should be inspired with an early admiration of Milton." The children's version aimed at making Milton less boring. Siddons responded to Dr. Johnson's complaint about the poem's "want of human interest" by focusing on those parts "which relate to the fate of our first parents" and by "omitting every thing, however exquisite in its kind, which did not immediately bear upon their affecting and important story" (Siddons, *Abridgement of Paradise Lost*, iii).

8. Randall McLeod, practicing a particularly artful form of textual analysis on one of Siddons's promptbooks, is able to determine how Siddons rearranged scenes in her reading of *King John*. He describes the promptbook as "all of her that remains to guide us through this dark evening, now the luminous sphere of Mrs Siddons has set" (Nimbus, "Evening without Mrs Siddons," 284). McLeod writes under the name of Claudia Nimbus in his essay "An Evening without Mrs Siddons." (The name "Claudia Nimbus"—along with McLeod's other avatar, "Random Cloud"—draws attention to how errors get introduced during textual transmission. McLeod's name morphs into contiguous versions of itself, as if some overtaxed scholar is free associating near matches: McLeod, Cloud, Nimbus.) McLeod urges his readers to take a tour "to the very sites where she inscribed, and pencilled and pinned—and riffled," insisting that the prompt book is "as close to The Tragic Muse as you will get, twilight revelation by bibliographic succession" (284).

I read McLeod's essay with a mixture of envy and chagrin because I knew that even if I studied Siddons's *King John* promptbook, I would not share McLeod's master lockpicker ability to make its tumblers line up and its doors swing open wide. The promptbook takes McLeod pretty close to Siddons—he creates an "apocalyptic rendering of Mrs Siddons' Book" that allows you to see the places where she folded back pages in order to get parts she didn't want to read out of the way—but it doesn't, alas, reveal how she sounded (283).

9. Sarah Siddons to Mrs. Fitz Hugh, 26 Jan. 1813, in Campbell, *Life of Mrs. Siddons*, 2: 346.

10. Campbell, *Life of Mrs. Siddons*, 2: 349. Siddons was appointed preceptress in English reading to the royal princesses in 1783, a dubious distinction, given that in 1783 there were five princesses ranging in age from six to seventeen, if you don't count the youngest, who was born that year. Siddons, by most reports, performed with aplomb when she read for the royal family. In *Reminiscences*, Siddons recalls that the king and queen expressed surprise at the equanimity she displayed at her first reading for royalty, but Siddons airily commented, "At any rate, I had frequently personated Queens" (22).

11. Frances Burney, from "Journal Letter to Susanna Phillips," 15 Aug. 1787, in Burney, *Journals and Letters*, 251.

12. Burney, "Journal Letter to Susanna Phillips," 251. Haydon, too, indicates that Siddons's stage persona infiltrated more casual encounters. He writes of visiting Mrs. Siddons with "something of the feeling of visiting Maria Theresa." Her voice, air, and actions were "calm and grand," having "something of a subdued feeling, as if she feared to speak too powerfully." Haydon goes on to say, "She seemed the Mother of the Gods, adapting her powers to converse with a mortal" (*Diary*, 2: 268).

13. For a discussion of Siddons's conversational lapses, see Patricia Howell Michaelson's *Speaking Volumes*, 117–23.

14. Joanna Baillie to Walter Scott, 28 Apr. 1813, *Further Letters of Joanna Baillie*, 53–54. I am grateful to Tom McLean for directing my attention to this letter in advance of his edition's publication.

15. Roach, "Public Intimacy," 26. See also Roach's analysis of the "it" factor, in *It*.

16. Baillie's comments are found in a letter that Anna Jameson included in a posthumous tribute to Siddons that was printed in *Visits and Sketches at Home and Abroad* (1834) and that is reprinted in the Broadview edition of Jameson's *Shakespeare's Heroines* (406).

17. Jameson, *Shakespeare's Heroines*, 406–7. Marvin Carlson's comments on aging actors shed some light on the range of responses to Siddons's very late performances: "Before we too hastily condemn the apparent folly and vanity of an aging actor still playing youthful roles, we must recall that every new performance of these roles will be ghosted by a theatrical recollection of the previous performances, so that audience reception of each new performance is conditioned by inevitable memories of this actor playing similar roles in the past. The voice that might seem to an outsider grown thin with age may still to a faithful public echo with the resonances of decades of theatregoing, that slightly bent body still be ghosted by years of memories of it in its full vigor" (*Haunted Stage*, 58).

CHAPTER THIRTEEN

1. Bell, "Prehistoric Telephone Days," 228.
2. Peters, "Helmholtz, Edison, and Sound History," 190.
3. As Mary Jacobus has taught us, *Macbeth* became particularly charged in the romantic period because of the way in which it mirrored the theatrical and politi-

cal concerns being enacted in the French Revolution—it became for romantic writers "a paradigm of their own unease about the power of the imagination" ("'That Great Stage Where Senators Perform,'" 37).

4. Charles H. Shattuck, introduction to *Macbeth*, in Kemble, *Promptbooks*, 5: i–ii.

5. *Macbeth*, in Kemble, *Promptbooks*, 5: 3.

6. *Macbeth*, in Kemble, *Promptbooks*, 5: 16.

7. Jenkin, *Mrs. Siddons as Lady Macbeth and as Queen Katharine*, 39 (hereafter cited in text).

8. Bell, Annotated Copy of Mrs. Inchbald's Edition of *The British Theatre*. Subsequent references to Bell's notes give page citations for the Jenkin transcription.

9. When Shelley read, his voice stopped being "dissonant, like a jarring string," nor did he read, as he spoke, "in sharp fourths, the most unpleasing sequence of sound that can fall on the human ear." While reading, Shelley "seemed . . . to have his voice under perfect command: it was good both in tune and in tone; it was low and soft, but clear, distinct, and expressive" (Peacock, *Memoirs of Percy Bysshe Shelley*, 55–56). My attention was drawn to this passage by David Perkins's "How the Romantics Recited Poetry."

10. This piece from the 26 Mar. 1810 *Edinburgh Courant* is gathered in James Ballantyne's *Characters by Mrs. Siddons* (19). When Kean played Richard in weak voice, the audience cried, "No, no," upon the announcement of the next night's performance. According to Hazlitt, they were in one accord regarding "the impropriety of requiring the repetition of this extraordinary effort, till every physical disadvantage had been completely removed" (*View of the English Stage*, 183).

11. Connor, *Dumbstruck*, 411 (hereafter cited in text).

12. Matthews, "Introduction," 19–20 (hereafter cited in text).

13. Jonathan Sterne argues that it is the very attempt to reproduce sound that introduces the concept of an "original" or "authentic" sound: "The original is itself an artifact of the process of reproduction. Without the technology of reproduction, the copies do not exist, but, then, neither would the originals" (*Audible Past*, 219).

CHAPTER FOURTEEN

1. Ockman and Silver, "Prologue: Sarah Bernhardt's Handkerchief," xv.

2. Holland, "Hearing the Dead," 255.

3. Holland, "Hearing the Dead," 248–49.

4. Campbell, *Life of Mrs. Siddons*, 2: 142.

5. Davis, "'Reading Shakespeare by Flashes of Lightning,'" 933.

6. Davis, "'Reading Shakespeare by Flashes of Lightning,'" 933–34.

7. It was analogous, Davis suggests, to "seeing the streets illuminated with coal gas light after groping around by moonlight and the occasional torch soaked in pitch" ("'Reading Shakespeare by Flashes of Lightning,'" 933).

8. Roach, *Cities of the Dead*, 80 and 78. On the question of what turns a theater actor into a phenomenon, see also Roach's *It*.

9. See Andrew Bennett, *Romantic Poets and the Culture of Posterity*.

10. "Ode: Intimations of Immortality," in *The Poetical Works of William Wordsworth*, 4: 280.

11. "Lines composed a few miles above Tintern Abbey," in *The Poetical Works of William Wordsworth*, 2: 261.

CHAPTER FIFTEEN

1. Hazlitt, "Mrs. Siddons's Lady Macbeth," 232.

2. Perhaps Severn was unusually sensitive to voices. He was also affected by the voice of a Miss Stephens, who sang "Angels ever bright and fair" over Queen Katherine's dying body. Charles Kean, years later, staged a striking visual tableau for this death scene, "with the groups of angels bearing palms, and with rays of heavenly light," but, for Severn, it could not compare in effect with "the solitary voice of Miss Stephens singing her sweet vibrating song" (Sharp, *Life and Letters of Joseph Severn*, 14n).

3. West, "Body Connoisseurship," 162.

4. *Times*, 29 Nov. 1811, qtd. in Bartholomeusz, *Winter's Tale in Performance*, 52.

5. Roach, "Patina," 196.

6. "Ode to a Nightingale," in Keats, *Complete Poems*, 281.

7. I am repeating here John Durham Peters's observation about Internet users in "Mass Media," 273.

8. The caption was actually "Ruth and Her New Cordless Telephone," and the cartoon gave Ruth a speech bubble that said "Nothing much. Standing in tears amid the alien corn." The online cartoon bank of the *New Yorker* magazine allowed me to establish that this incorrectly recalled cartoon was the work of J. B. Handelsman, and that it appeared in the 25 Sept. 1989 issue.

9. John Picker provided me with this detail about Edison's romantic poetry appropriation. See *Victorian Soundscapes*, 116. See also Jason Camlot's discussion of this aspect of Edison's marketing strategy in "Early Talking Books."

10. Qtd. in Andrews, *Edison Phonograph*, xiv-xv.

11. John Durham Peters writes, "Both sound recording and alphabetic writing lifted old limits that held voices in check—distance, dissipation, and discretion. A captured voice forfeits its body, mortality, and authorial control. With the ability to record, amplify, and transmit sound by machines, the voice apparently lost its finitude" ("Helmholtz, Edison, and Sound History," 178).

12. Jody Rosen, "Researchers Play Tune Recorded Before Edison."

13. Babbage, *Ninth Bridgewater Treatise*, 113 and 109-17.

14. Pierce, *The Collected Papers*, 5: 543. John Peters brought this passage to my attention.

Bibliography

Abdy, Jane. "Sarah Bernhardt and Lalique: A Confusion of Evidence." *Apollo* 125, no. 303 (1987): 325–30.

"Abstract of the Registry Kept at the Lying-in Hospital, in Dublin." *Provincial Medical and Surgical Journal* 1 (31 Oct. 1840): 87.

Andrews, Frank. *The Edison Phonograph: The British Connection.* Rugby: The City of London Phonograph and Gramophone Society, 1986.

Ashton, Geoffrey. *Pictures in the Garrick Club.* Edited by Kalman A. Burnim and Andrew Wilton. London: Garrick Club, 1997.

Asleson, Robyn, ed. *Notorious Muse: The Actress in British Art and Culture, 1776–1812.* New Haven: Yale University Press, 2003.

Asleson, Robyn, ed. *A Passion for Performance: Sarah Siddons and Her Portraitists.* Los Angeles: The J. Paul Getty Museum, 1999.

Asleson, Robyn. "'She Was Tragedy Personified': Crafting the Siddons Legend in Art and Life." In *A Passion for Performance: Sarah Siddons and Her Portraitists,* edited by Robyn Asleson. Los Angeles: The J. Paul Getty Museum, 1999.

Austin, Gilbert. *Chironomia; or, A Treatise on Rhetorical Delivery.* London: T. Cadell and W. Davies, 1806.

Babbage, Charles. *The Ninth Bridgewater Treatise.* London: John Murray, 1837.

Backscheider, Paula R. *Spectacular Politics: Theatrical Power and Mass Culture in Early Modern England.* Baltimore: Johns Hopkins University Press, 1993.

Baer, Marc. *Theatre and Disorder in Late Georgian London.* Oxford: Clarendon Press, 1992.

Baillie, Joanna. *The Collected Letters of Joanna Baillie.* Edited by Judith Bailey Slagle. Madison, N.J.: Fairleigh Dickinson University Press, 1999.

Baillie, Joanna. *Further Letters of Joanna Baillie.* Edited by Thomas McLean. Madison, N.J.: Fairleigh Dickinson University Press, 2010.

Baillie, Joanna. "To the Reader." In *A Series of Plays.* 3 vols. New York: Garland Publishing, 1977. 3:iii–xxxi.

Ballantyne, James. *Characters by Mrs. Siddons.* Edinburgh, 1812.

Balme, Christopher. "Cultural Anthropology and Theatre Historiography: Notes on a Methodological Rapprochement." *Theatre Survey* 35 (1994): 33–52.

Bancroft, Squire. *Mr. and Mrs. Bancroft On and Off the Stage.* London: Richard Bentley and Son, 1888.

Barish, Jonas A. *The Antitheatrical Prejudice.* Berkeley: University of California Press, 1981.

Barthes, Roland. "The Grain of the Voice." In *The Responsibility of Forms*, translated by Richard Howard. New York: Hill and Wang, 1985. 267–77.

Barthes, Roland. "Inaugural Lecture, Collège de France." Translated by Richard Howard. In *A Barthes Reader*, edited by Susan Sontag. New York: Hill and Wang, 1982. 457–78.

Barthes, Roland. "The Phantoms of the Opera." In *The Grain of the Voice: Interviews 1962–1980*, translated by Linda Coverdale. New York: Hill and Wang, 1985. 183–87.

Bartholomeusz, Dennis. *The Winter's Tale in Performance in England and America, 1611–1976.* Cambridge: Cambridge University Press, 1982.

Bate, Jonathan. "Shakespeare and the Rival Muses: Siddons versus Jordan." In *Notorious Muse: The Actress in British Art and Culture, 1776–1812*, edited by Robyn Asleson. New Haven: Yale University Press, 2003.

The Beauties of Mrs. Siddons: or a Review of her Performance of the Characters of Belvidera, Zara, Isabella, . . . in Letters from a Lady of Distinction. London: John Strahan, 1786.

Bell, Alexander Graham. "Prehistoric Telephone Days." *National Geographic Magazine* 41, no. 3 (1922): 223–41.

Bell, George Joseph. Annotated Copy of Mrs. Inchbald's edition of *The British Theatre*, ca. 1806. Folger Shakespeare Library. W.a. 70–72.

Belton, Fred. *Random Recollections of an Old Actor.* London: Tinsley Brothers, 1880.

Benjamin, Walter. "The Work of Art in the Age of Its Technological Reproducibility." In *Walter Benjamin: Selected Writings*, vol. 3, edited by Howard Eiland and Michael W. Jennings, translated by Edmund Jephcott and Harry Zohn. Cambridge: Harvard University Press, 2002. 101–33.

Bennett, Alan. *The History Boys.* London: Faber and Faber, 2004.

Bennett, Andrew. *Romantic Poets and the Culture of Posterity.* New York: Cambridge University Press, 1999.

Bennett, Shelley, and Mark Leonard. "'A Sublime and Masterly Performance': The Making of Joshua Reynolds's *Sarah Siddons as the Tragic Muse*." In *A Passion for Performance: Sarah Siddons and Her Portraitists*, edited by Robyn Asleson. Los Angeles: The J. Paul Getty Museum, 1999. 97–140.

Bernhardt, Sarah. *Phèdre* recording (1910). Cylinder Preservation and Digitization Project. University of California, Santa Barbara. Available at http://cylinders .library.ucsb.edu

Berry, Francis. *Poetry and the Physical Voice.* New York: Oxford University Press, 1962.

Blesser, Barry, and Linda-Ruth Salter. *Spaces Speak, Are You Listening? Experiencing Aural Architecture.* Cambridge: MIT Press, 2007.

Bloom, Gina. *Voice in Motion: Staging Gender, Shaping Sound in Early Modern England.* Philadelphia: University of Pennsylvania Press, 2007.

Boaden, James, ed. *Memoirs of Mrs. Siddons.* 2 vols. London: Henry Colburn, 1827.

Boaden, James, ed. *Memoirs of the Life of John Philip Kemble, Esq.* 2 vols. London: Longman, Hurst, Rees, Orme, Brown, and Green, 1825.

Boucicault, Dion. *The Art of Acting.* New York: Columbia University Press, 1926.

Bratton, Jacky. *New Readings in Theatre History.* Cambridge: Cambridge University Press, 2003.

Bratton, Jacky, Gilli Bush-Bailey, and DT2323A Semester 97/8B. "The Management of Laughter: Jane Scott's *Camilla the Amazon* in 1998." In *Women in British Romantic Theatre: Drama, Performance, and Society, 1790–1840,* edited by Catherine Burroughs. Cambridge: Cambridge University Press, 2000. 178–206.

Brownstein, Rachel M. *Tragic Muse: Rachel of the Comédie Française.* New York: Knopf, 1993.

Buchanan, Lindal. "Sarah Siddons and Her Place in Rhetorical History." *Rhetorica* 25 (2007): 413–34.

Burney, Frances. *Journals and Letters.* Edited by Peter Sabor and Lars E. Troide. London: Penguin Books, 2001.

Burnim, Kalman A. *David Garrick, Director.* Pittsburgh: University of Pittsburgh Press, 1961.

Burnim, Kalman A., ed. "The Letters of Sarah and William Siddons to Hester Lynch Piozzi in the John Rylands Library." *Bulletin of the John Rylands Library* 52 (Autumn 1969): 46–95.

Burroughs, Catherine, ed. *Women in British Romantic Theatre: Drama, Performance, and Society, 1790–1840.* Cambridge: Cambridge University Press, 2000.

Burwick, Frederick. "The Ideal Shatters: Sarah Siddons, Madness, and the Dynamics of Gesture." In *Notorious Muse: The Actress in British Art and Culture, 1776–1812,* edited by Robyn Asleson. New Haven: Yale University Press, 2003. 129–50.

Byron, George Gordon. *Byron's Letters and Journals.* Edited by Leslie A. Marchand. Cambridge: Harvard University Press, 1973–94.

Camlot, Jason. "Early Talking Books: Spoken Recordings and Recitation Anthologies, 1880–1920." *Book History* 6 (2003): 147–73.

Campbell, Thomas. *Life of Mrs. Siddons.* 2 vols. London: Effingham Wilson, 1834.

Carlson, Julie A. *In the Theatre of Romanticism: Coleridge, Nationalism, Women.* New York: Cambridge University Press, 1994.

Carlson, Marvin. *The Haunted Stage: The Theatre as Memory Machine.* Ann Arbor: University of Michigan Press, 2001.

Case, Sue-Ellen. "Theatre/History/Revolution." In *Critical Theory and Performance,* edited by Janelle G. Reinelt and Joseph R. Roach. Ann Arbor: University of Michigan Press, 1992. 418–29.

A Catalogue of the Excellent Household Furniture, a Small Library of Books, Paintings, Wines and Sundry Effects, Late the Genuine Property of Mrs. Siddons. London: Hewlett and Brimmer, [1831]. This document survives in the Harvard Theatre Collection.

Coleridge, Samuel Taylor. *The Collected Works of Samuel Taylor Coleridge*, 16: I pt. 2. Edited by J. C. C. Mays. Princeton: Princeton University Press, 2001.

Collins, Philip. *Reading Aloud: A Victorian Métier*. Lincoln, England: The Tennyson Society, 1972.

Connor, Steven. *Dumbstruck: A Cultural History of Ventriloquism*. Oxford: Oxford University Press, 2000.

Connor, Steven. "Voice, Technology and the Victorian Era." Paper delivered at the Conference on Science and Culture 1780–1900. Birckbeck College, London. 12 September 1997. Available at http://www.stevenconnor.com/phones.htm.

Conway, Jeffery, Lynn Crosbie, and David Trinidad. *Phoebe 2002: An Essay in Verse*. New York: Turtle Point Press, 2003.

Corbin, Alain. *Village Bells: Sound and Meaning in the 19th-Century Countryside*. Translated by Martin Thom. New York: Columbia University Press, 1998.

Crary, Jonathan. *Techniques of the Observer: On Vision and Modernity in the Nineteenth Century*. Cambridge: MIT Press, 1990.

Davis, Tracy C., ed. *The Cambridge Companion to Performance Studies*. New York: Cambridge University Press, 2008.

Davis, Tracy C. "'Reading Shakespeare by Flashes of Lightning': Challenging the Foundations of Romantic Acting Theory." *ELH* 62 (1995): 933–54.

Denby, David. "Big Pictures: Hollywood Looks for a Future." *New Yorker*, 8 January 2007, 54–63.

Dimock, Wai Chee. "A Theory of Resonance." *PMLA* 112 (1997): 1060–71.

Dolar, Mladen. *A Voice and Nothing More*. Cambridge.: MIT Press, 2006.

Donaldson, Frances. *The Actor-Managers*. Chicago: Henry Regnery Company, 1970.

Donaldson, W. *Fifty Years of Green-Room Gossip*. London: John and Robert Maxwell, 1881.

Donohue, Joseph. "Evidence and Documentation." In *Interpreting the Theatrical Past: Essays in the Historiography of Performance*, edited by Thomas Postlewait and Bruce A. McConachie. Iowa City: University of Iowa Press, 1989. 177–97.

Donkin, Ellen. "Mrs. Siddons Looks Back in Anger: Feminist Historiography for Eighteenth-Century British Theater." In *Critical Theory and Performance*, edited by Janelle G. Reinelt and Joseph R. Roach. Ann Arbor: University of Michigan Press, 1992. 276–90.

Downer, Alan S. "Nature to Advantage Dressed: Eighteenth-Century Acting." *PMLA* 58 (1943): 1002–37.

Downer, Alan S. "Players and Painted Stage: Nineteenth-Century Acting." *PMLA* 61 (1946): 522–76.

Dunsby, Jonathan. "Roland Barthes and the Grain of Panzéra's Voice." *Journal of the Royal Musical Association* 134, no. 1 (2009): 113–32.

Dyer, Geoff. *The Missing of the Somme*. London: Hamish Hamilton, 1994.

Edison, Thomas. *The Diary and Sundry Observations of Thomas Alva Edison*. Edited by Dagobert D. Runes. New York: Greenwood Press, Publishers, 1968.

Edison, Thomas. "The Phonograph and Its Future." *North American Review* 262 (May–June 1878): 527–36.

Edwards, Jason. "Thomas Dermody." In *Oxford Dictionary of National Biography*, online edition.

Elfenbein, Andrew. *Romanticism and the Rise of English*. Stanford: Stanford University Press, 2008.

Enfield, William. *Exercises in Elocution*. London: J. Johnson, 1780.

Enfield, William. *The Speaker*. London: Joseph Johnson, 1774.

Engel, Laura. "The Personating of Queens: Lady Macbeth, Sarah Siddons, and the Creation of Female Celebrity in the Late Eighteenth Century." In *Macbeth: New Critical Essays*, edited by Nick Moschovakis. New York: Routledge, 2008. 240–57.

Feinstein, Robert. "Sarah Bernhardt and the Bettini Recording Legacy." *In the Groove* (newsletter of the Michigan Antique Phonograph Society), Feb. 2002.

Fitzgerald, Percy. *The Kembles*. 2 vols. London: Tinsley Brothers, 1871.

Foster, Susan Leigh. "Movement's Contagion: The Kinesthetic Impact of Performance." In *The Cambridge Companion to Performance Studies*, edited by Tracy Davis. New York: Cambridge University Press, 2008. 46–59.

Freud, Sigmund. *Letters of Sigmund Freud*. Edited by Ernest L. Freud. Translated by Tania and James Stern. New York: Basic Books, 1960.

Galindo, Catherine. *Mrs. Galindo's Letter to Mrs. Siddons*. London: Printed for the Authoress, 1809.

Galperin, William H. *The Return of the Visible in British Romanticism*. Baltimore: Johns Hopkins University Press, 1993.

Gaull, Marilyn. "Romantic Theatre." *Wordsworth Circle* 14 (1983): 255–63.

Gitelman, Lisa. *Always Already New: Media, History, and the Data of Culture*. Cambridge: MIT Press, 2006.

Gold, Arthur. *The Divine Sarah*. New York: Alfred A. Knopf, 1991.

Goodman, Lizbeth, and Jane De Gay, eds. *The Routledge Reader in Politics and Performance*. New York: Routledge, 2000.

Gosse, Edmund. "Sarah Siddons." *Century Illustrated Monthly Magazine* 46 (July 1893): 380–83.

Great Historical Shakespeare Recordings. Naxos Audio Books, 2000.

Grover-Friedlander, Michal. "The Afterlife of Maria Callas's Voice." *Musical Quarterly* 88 (2005): 35–62.

Grover-Friedlander, Michal. *Vocal Apparitions: The Attraction of Cinema to Opera*. Princeton: Princeton University Press, 2005.

Haslewood, Joseph. *The Secret History of the Green Rooms*. 2 vols. London: J. Ridgway, 1790.

Hatton, Joseph. "An Irving Reminiscence." In *In Jest and Earnest: A Book of Gossip*. London: Leadenhall, 1893. 135–37.

Haydon, Benjamin Robert. *The Diary of Benjamin Robert Haydon*. 5 vols. Edited by Willard Bissell Pope. Cambridge: Harvard University Press, 1960.

Hazlitt, William. "Miss O'Neill's Juliet." In *The Complete Works of William Hazlitt*, vol. 5. Edited by P. P. Howe, 1930–34. Reprint, New York: AMS Press, 1967. 198–200.

Hazlitt, William. "Mrs. Siddons." In *The Complete Works of William Hazlett*, vol. 18. Edited by P. P. Howe. 1930–34. Reprint, New York: AMS Press, 1967. 406–10.

Hazlitt, William. "Mrs. Siddons's Lady Macbeth." In *The Complete Works of William Hazlett*, vol. 18. Edited by P. P. Howe. 1930–34. Reprint, New York: AMS Press, 1967. 232–33.

Hazlitt, William. Review of "Christabel" in *The Examiner*, 2 June 1816. Reprinted in *The Romantics Reviewed*, part A, vol. 2. Edited by Donald Reiman. New York: Garland Publishing, 1972. 530–31.

Hazlitt, William. *A View of the English Stage*. In *The Complete Works of William Hazlitt*, vol. 5. Edited by P. P. Howe. 1930–34. Reprint, New York: AMS Press, 1967. 163–379.

Hazlitt, William. "The Winter's Tale." In *The Complete Works of William Hazlitt*, vol. 4. Edited by P. P. Howe. 1930–34. Reprint, New York: AMS Press, 1967. 324–29.

Highfill, Philip H., Jr., Kalman A. Burnim, and Edward A. Langhans, eds. *A Biographical Dictionary of Actors, Actresses, Musicians, Dancers, Managers and Other Stage Personnel in London, 1660–1800*. 16 vols. Carbondale: Southern Illinois University Press, 1973–93.

Hogan, Charles Beecher. Introduction to *The London Stage 1660–1800*, part 5: 1776–1800. Edited by Charles Beecher Hogan. Carbondale: Southern Illinois University Press, 1968.

Hogg, Thomas Jefferson. "The Life of Shelley." In *The Life of Percy Bysshe Shelley*, 2 vols. Edited by Humbert Wolfe. London: J. M. Dent, 1933.

Holcroft, Thomas. *Alwyn: or The Gentleman Comedian*. In *The Novels and Selected Plays of Thomas Holcroft*, vol. 1. Edited by Rick Incorvati. London: Pickering and Chatto, 2007.

Holland, Peter. "Hearing the Dead: The Sound of David Garrick." In *Players, Playwrights, Playhouses: Investigating Performance, 1660–1800*, edited by Michael Cordner and Peter Holland. New York: Palgrave Macmillan, 2007. 248–70.

Holland, Peter. "A History of Histories: From Flecknoe to Nicoll." In *Theorizing Practice: Redefining Theater History*, edited by W. B. Worthen and Peter Holland. New Year: Palgrave Macmillan, 2003. 8–29.

Holmes, Richard. *Shelley: The Pursuit*. London: Weidenfeld and Nicolson, 1974.

Howard, Tony. *Women as Hamlet: Performance and Interpretation in Theatre, Film and Fiction*. Cambridge: Cambridge University Press, 2007.

Hume, Robert D. "Theatre History, 1660–1800: Aims, Materials, Methodology." In *Players, Playwrights, Playhouses: Investigating Performance, 1660–1800*, edited by Michael Cordner and Peter Holland. New York: Palgrave Macmillan, 2007. 9–44.

Hunter, J. Paul. "Sleeping Beauties: Are Historical Aesthetics Worth Recovering?" *Eighteenth-Century Studies* 34, no. 1 (2000): 1–20.

Inchbald, Elizabeth, ed. "Remarks." In *Isabella; or, The Fatal Marriage* by Thomas Southern. Vol. 7 of *The British Theatre*. Edited by Elizabeth Inchbald. London: Longman, Hurst, Rees, and Orme, 1808. 3–5.

Inchbald, Elizabeth. "Remarks." In *The Merchant of Venice* by William Shakespeare. Vol. 2 of *The British Theatre*. Edited by Elizabeth Inchbald. London: Longman, Hurst, Rees, and Orme, 1808. 3–5.

Jacobus, Mary. " 'That Great Stage Where Senators Perform': Macbeth and the Politics of Romantic Theatre." In *Romanticism, Writing and Sexual Difference.* Oxford: Clarendon Press, 1989. 33–68.

James, Henry. *The Aspern Papers.* Vol. 12 of *The Novels and Tales of Henry James.* 1908. Reprint, New York: August M. Kelley, 1971.

Jameson, Anna Murphy. *Shakespeare's Heroines.* Edited by Cheri L. Larsen Hoeckley. Peterloo, Ont.: Broadview Press, 2005.

Jenkin, H. C. Fleeming. *Mrs. Siddons as Lady Macbeth and as Queen Katharine.* New York: Dramatic Museum of Columbia University, 1915.

Jones, J. Jennifer. "Sounds Romantic: The Castrato and English Poetics Around 1800." Romantic Circles. *Opera and Romanticism.* Praxis Series. Edited by Gillen D'Arcy Wood. Available at http://www.rc.umd.edu/praxis/opera/jones/jones.html [accessed 25 November 2005]

Keats, John. *John Keats: Complete Poems.* Edited by Jack Stillinger. Cambridge: Harvard University Press, 1978.

Kemble, Frances Ann. *Record of a Girlhood.* 3 vols. London: Richard Bentley and Son, 1878.

Kemble, John Philip. *John Philip Kemble Promptbooks.* 11 vols. Edited by Charles H. Shattuck. Charlottesville: University Press of Virginia, 1974.

Kennard, Nina. *Mrs. Siddons.* Boston: Roberts Brothers, 1887.

Kennedy, Dennis. "Confessions of an Encyclopedist." In *Theorizing Practice: Redefining Theatre History,* edited by W. B. Worthen and Peter Holland. New York: Palgrave Macmillan, 2003. 30–46.

Kershaw, Baz. "Performance as Research: Live Events and Documents." In *The Cambridge Companion to Performance Studies,* edited by Tracy Davis. New York: Cambridge University Press, 2008. 23–46.

Kilgarriff, Michael. "Henry Irving and the Phonograph: Bennett Maxwell." Irving Society. Available at http://theirvingsociety.org.uk.

Kittler, Friedrich A. *Gramophone, Film, Typewriter.* Translated by Geoffrey Winthrop-Young and Michael Wutz. Stanford: Stanford University Press, 1999.

Kittler, Friedrich A. *Literature, Media, Information Systems.* Edited by John Johnston. New York: Routledge, 1997.

Kittler, Friedrich A. "Man as a Drunken Town-Musician." *MLN* 118 (April 2003): 637–52.

Koestenbaum, Wayne. *The Queen's Throat: Opera, Homosexuality and the Mystery of Desire.* New York: Penguin Books, 1993.

Lamb, Charles. "A Chapter on Ears." In *Elia. The Works of Charles and Mary Lamb,* vol. 2. Edited by E. V. Lucas, 1903. 38–41.

Lamb, Charles. "On the Tragedies of Shakspeare, Considered with Reference to Their Fitness for Stage Representation." In *The Works of Charles and Mary Lamb,* vol. 1. Edited by E. V. Lucas. 1903. Reprint, New York: AMS Press, 1968. 97–111.

Lamb, Charles, and Mary Lamb. *Tales from Shakespeare.* Vol. 3 of *The Works of Charles and Mary Lamb.* Edited by E. V. Lucas. 1903. Reprint, New York: AMS Press, 1968. 1–206.

Langan, Celeste. "Understanding Media in 1805: Audiovisual Hallucination in *The Lay of the Last Minstrel.*" *Studies in Romanticism* 40 (Spring 2001): 49–70.

Langan, Celeste, and Maureen N. McLane. "The Medium of Romantic Poetry." In *The Cambridge Companion to British Romantic Poetry*, edited by James Chandler and Maureen N. McLane. New York: Cambridge University Press, 2008. 239–62.

Leigh-Johnson, Judy. "Voice for Actors." Class lecture. University of Iowa, May 2005.

Levitov, Karen. "The Divine Sarah and the Infernal Sally: Bernhardt in the Words of Her Contemporaries." In *Sarah Bernhardt: The Art of High Drama*, edited by Carol Ockman and Kenneth E. Silver. New Haven: Yale University Press, 2005. 125–43.

Luckhurst, Mary, and Jane Moody, eds. *Theatre and Celebrity in Britain, 1660–2000.* New York: Palgrave Macmillan, 2005.

Macaulay, Alastair. "Laughter beyond Bracknell." *Times Literary Supplement*, 29 September 2006, 18–19.

Macdonald, E. L., and Kathleen Scherf. Introduction to *The Vampyre: A Tale and Ernestus Berchtold or, The Modern Oedipus*, by John William Polidori. Edited by D. L. Macdonald and Kathleen Scherf. Petersborough, Ont.: Broadview, 2008. 9–32.

Manning, Peter J. "'The Birthday of Typography': A Response to Celeste Langan." *Studies in Romanticism* 40 (Spring 2001): 71–83.

Manning, Peter J. "Manufacturing the Romantic Image: Hazlitt and Coleridge Lecturing." In *Romantic Metropolis: The Urban Scene of British Culture, 1780–1840*, edited by James Chandler and Kevin Gilmartin. Cambridge: Cambridge University Press, 2005.

Manning, Peter J. "'Will No One Tell Me What She Sings?': *The Solitary Reaper* and the Contexts of Criticism." In *Reading Romantics: Texts and Contexts*. New York: Oxford University Press, 1990. 241–72.

Manvell, Roger. *Sarah Siddons: Portrait of an Actress.* New York: G. P. Putnam's Sons, 1971.

Matthews, Brander. "Introduction." In *Mrs. Siddons as Lady Macbeth and as Queen Katharine*, by H. C. Fleeming Jenkin. New York: Dramatic Museum of Columbia University, 1915. 1–24.

McKellen, Ian. Foreword to *The Right to Speak*, by Patsy Rodenburg. New York: Routledge, 1992. vi–viii.

McLuhan, Marshall. *Understanding Media: The Extensions of Man.* New York: McGraw Hill, 1964.

McPherson, Heather. "Siddons Redivia: Death, Memory and Theatrical Afterlife." In *Romanticism and Celebrity Culture, 1750–1850*, edited by Tom Mole. New York: Cambridge University Press, 2009. 120–40.

McPherson, Sue, and Julia Swindells, eds. *Women's Theatrical Memoirs.* 10 vols. London: Pickering and Chatto, 2007–8.

Medwin, Thomas. *Journal of the Conversations of Lord Byron.* London: Henry Colburn, 1824.

Medwin, Thomas. *The Life of Percy Bysshe Shelley*. 1913. Reprint, St. Clair Shores, Mich.: Scholarly Press, 1971.

Menefee, David W. *Sarah Bernhardt in the Theatre of Films and Sound Recordings*. Jefferson, N.C.: McFarland and Company, Inc., Publishers, 2003.

Michaelson, Patricia Howell. *Speaking Volumes: Women, Reading, and Speech in the Age of Austen*. Stanford: Stanford University Press, 2002.

The Modern Stage Exemplified, in an Epistle to a Young Actor. London: W. Flexney, 1788.

Molloy, J. Fitzgerald. Introduction to *Memoirs of Mary Robinson*. London: Gibbings and Company, 1895.

Murdoch, James E. *The Stage, or, Recollections of Actors and Acting*. Philadelphia: J. M. Stoddart and Co., 1880.

Nicoll, Allardyce. *A History of English Drama 1660–1900*. 6 vols. Cambridge: Cambridge University Press, 1966.

Nimbus, Claudia [Randall McLeod]. "An Evening without Mrs Siddons." *Critical Survey* 7, no. 3 (1995): 256–91.

Observations on Mrs. Siddons in the Following Characters: Margaret of Anjou, Belvidera, Jane Shore, Lady Randolph, Isabella, Zara, Euphrasia, and Zara in the Mourning Bride. Dublin: P. Byrne, 1784.

Ockman, Carol. "Was She Magnificent? Sarah Bernhardt's Reach." In *Sarah Bernhardt: The Art of High Drama*, edited by Carol Ockman and Kenneth Silver. New Haven: Yale University Press, 2005. 23–74.

Ockman, Carol, and Kenneth Silver. "Prologue: Sarah Bernhardt's Handkerchief." In *Sarah Bernhardt: The Art of High Drama*, edited by Carol Ockman and Kenneth Silver. New Haven: Yale University Press, 2005. xiv.

Ockman, Carol, and Kenneth Silver, eds. *Sarah Bernhardt: The Art of High Drama*. New Haven: Yale University Press, 2005.

O'Keefe, John. *Edwin's Pills to Purge Melancholy*. 3rd ed. London, 1789.

Orgel, Stephen. Introduction to William Shakespeare's *The Winter's Tale*, edited by Stephen Orgel. Oxford: Clarendon Press, 1996. 1–83.

Otway, Thomas. *Venice Preserved*. Edited by Malcolm Kelsall. Lincoln: University of Nebraska Press, 1969.

Oya, Reiko. *Representing Shakespearean Tragedy: Garrick, the Kembles, and Kean*. Cambridge: Cambridge University Press, 2007.

Pakenham, Simona. *Cheltenham: A Biography*. London: Macmillan, 1971.

Papendiek, Charlotte Louise Henrietta. *Court and Private Life in the Time of Queen Charlotte*. London: R. Bentley and Son, 1887.

Parsons, Mrs. Clement (Florence Mary Wilson Parsons). *The Incomparable Siddons*. 1909. Reprint, Freeport, NY: Books for Libraries Press, 1970.

Pascoe, Judith. *Romantic Theatricality: Gender, Poetry, and Spectatorship*. Ithaca: Cornell University Press, 1997.

Peacock, Thomas Love. *Memoirs of Percy Bysshe Shelley*. In *The Works of Thomas Love Peacock*, vol. 8. London: Constable, 1934.

Peake, Richard Brinsley. *Memoirs of the Colman Family*. 2 vols. London: Richard Bentley, 1841.

Pearson, Roberta E. *Eloquent Gestures: The Transformation of Performance Style in the Griffith Biograph Films*. Berkeley: University of California Press, 1992.

Peirce, Charles Sanders. *The Collected Papers of Charles Sanders Peirce*. 8 vols. Edited by Charles Hartshorne and Paul Weiss. Cambridge: Harvard University Press, 1931–58.

Perkins, David. "How the Romantics Recited Poetry." *SEL* 31 (1991): 655–71.

Peters, John Durham. "Helmholz, Edison, and Sound History." In *Memory Bytes: History, Technology, and Digital Culture*, edited by Lauren Rabinovitz and Abraham Geil. Durham: Duke University Press, 2004. 177–98.

Peters, John Durham. "Mass Media." In *Critical Terms for Media Studies*, edited by W. J. T. Mitchell and Mark B. N. Hansen. Chicago: University of Chicago Press, 2010. 266–79.

Peters, John Durham. *Speaking into the Air: A History of the Idea of Communication*. Chicago: University of Chicago Press, 1999.

Phelan, Peggy. *Unmarked: The Politics of Performance*. New York: Routledge, 1993.

"The Phonograph and Its Improvements." *Frank Leslie's Weekly*, 3 March 1892, 82–83.

Picker, John M. *Victorian Soundscapes*. Oxford: Oxford University Press, 2003.

Poizat, Michel. *The Angel's Cry: Beyond the Pleasure Principle in Opera*. Trans. Arthur Denner. Ithaca: Cornell University Press, 1992.

Polanski, Roman. *The Tragedy of Macbeth*. VHS. Sony Pictures Home Entertainment, 1971.

Polidori, John William. *The Diary of Dr. John William Polidori 1816*. Edited by William Michael Rossetti. London: Elkin Mathews, 1911.

Polidori, John William. *The Vampyre: A Tale and Ernestus Berchtoldi; or the Modern Oedipus*. Edited by D. L. MacDonald and Kathleen Scherf. Petersborough, Ont.: Broadview, 2008.

Postlewait, Thomas, and Bruce A. McConachie, eds. *Interpreting the Theatrical Past: Essays in the Historiography of Performance*. Iowa City: University of Iowa Press, 1989.

Price, Leah. *The Anthology and the Rise of the Novel*. New York: Cambridge, 2000.

Radcliffe, Ann. "On the Supernatural in Poetry." *New Monthly Magazine* 16, no. 1 (1826): 145–52.

Rath, Richard Cullen. *How Early America Sounded*. Ithaca: Cornell University Press, 2003.

Reiman, Donald H., ed. *The Romantics Reviewed*. Vol. 2. New York: Garland Publishing, Inc., 1972.

Reinelt, Janelle G., and Joseph R. Roach, eds. *Critical Theory and Performance*. Ann Arbor: University of Michigan Press, 1992.

Reinelt, Janelle G. Introduction to "Semiotics and Deconstruction," in *Critical Theory in Performance*, edited by Janelle G. Reinelt and Joseph R. Roach. Ann Arbor: University of Michigan Press, 1992. 109–16.

Ribeiro, Aileen. "Costuming the Part: A Discourse of Fashion and Fiction in the Image of the Actress in England, 1776–1812." In *Notorious Muse: The Actress in British Art and Culture 1776–1812*, edited by Robyn Asleson. New Haven: Yale University Press, 2003. 104–28.

Richards, Sandra. *The Rise of the English Actress*. New York: St. Martin's Press, 1993.

Roach, Joseph R. *Cities of the Dead: Circum-Atlantic Performance*. New York: Columbia University Press, 1996.

Roach, Joseph R. Introduction to "Theater History and Historiography." In *Critical Theory and Performance*, edited by Janelle G. Reinelt and Joseph R. Roach. Ann Arbor: University of Michigan Press, 1992. 293–98.

Roach, Joseph R. *It*. Ann Arbor: University of Michigan Press, 2007.

Roach, Joseph R. "Patina: Mrs Siddons and the Depth of Surfaces." In *Notorious Muse: The Actress in British Art and Culture, 1776–1812*, edited by Robyn Asleson. New Haven: Yale University Press, 2003. 195–210.

Roach, Joseph R. *The Player's Passion: Studies in the Science of Acting*. Newark: University of Delaware Press, 1985.

Roach, Joseph R. "Public Intimacy: The Prior History of 'It.'" In *Theatre and Celebrity in Britain, 1660–2000*, edited by Mary Luckhurst and Jane Moody. New York: Palgrave Macmillan, 2005. 15–30.

Robinson, Henry Crabb. *The London Theatre 1811–1866*. Edited by Eluned Brown. London: The Society for Theatre Research, 1966.

Rodenburg, Patsy. *The Right to Speak*. New York: Routledge, 1992.

Rogers, Pat. "'Towering Beyond Her Sex': Stature and Sublimity in the Achievement of Sarah Siddons." In *Curtain Calls*, edited by Mary Anne Schofield and Cecilia Macheski. Athens: Ohio University Press, 1991. 48–67.

Rosen, Jody. "Researchers Play Tune Recorded Before Edison." *New York Times*, 27 March 2008, online edition. [accessed 26 August 2008].

Rovee, Christopher. "'Everybody's Shakespeare': Representative Genres and John Boydell's *Winter's Tale*." *Studies in Romanticism* 41 (Winter 2002): 509–43.

Royde-Smith, Naomi. *The Private Life of Mrs. Siddons: A Psychological Investigation*. London: Victor Gollancz, 1933.

Russett, Margaret. "Meter, Identity, Voice: Untranslating *Christabel*." *SEL* 43 (2003): 773–97.

Sarlós, Robert K. "Performance Reconstruction: The Vital Link between Past and Future." In *Interpreting the Theatrical Past: Essays in the Historiography of Performance*, edited by Thomas Postlewait and Bruce A. McConachie. Iowa City: University of Iowa Press, 1989. 198–229.

Saunders, George. *A Treatise on Theatres*. London, 1790.

Schroeder, Janice. "Speaking Volumes: Victorian Feminism and the Appeal of Public Discussion." *Nineteenth-Century Contexts* 25 (2003): 97–117.

Scott, Walter. Essay on Drama. In *The Miscellaneous Prose Works of Sir Walter Scott*, vol. 6. Edinburgh: Cadell and Co., 1827.

Seward, Anna. *The Letters of Anna Seward: Written between the Years 1784 and 1807*. 6 vols. Edinburgh: A. Constable, 1811.

Seward, Anna. *The Swan of Lichfield*. Edited by Hesketh Pearson. London: Hamish Hamilton, 1936.

Shakespeare, William. *Macbeth*. Edited by Nicholas Brooke. Oxford: Oxford University Press, 1994.

Shakespeare, William. *Macbeth*. With Jane Lapotaire as Lady Macbeth. Directed by Jack Gold. DVD. BBC. Ambrose Video, 1978.

Shakespeare, William. *Macbeth.* With Jeanette Nolan as Lady Macbeth. Directed by Orson Welles. 1948. VHS. Republic Pictures, 1998.

Shakespeare, William. *Macbeth.* With Fiona Shaw as Lady Macbeth. CD. Classical Recording Company. Naxos Audio Books, 2005.

Sharp, William. *The Life and Letters of Joseph Severn.* New York: Charles Scribner's Sons, 1892.

Shaughnessy, Robert. "Sarah Siddons." In *Oxford Dictionary of National Biography,* online edition.

Sheridan, Thomas. *A Course of Lectures on Elocution.* 1762. Reprint, New York: Benjamin Blom, 1968.

The Siddoniad: A Characteristical and Critical Poem. Dublin: R. Marchibank, 1784.

Siddons, Henry. *Practical Illustrations of Rhetorical Gesture and Action; Adapted to the English Drama.* London: Richard Phillips, 1807.

Siddons, Sarah. *An Abridgement of Paradise Lost.* London: John Murray, 1822.

Siddons, Sarah. Manuscript copy of *Paradise Lost.* Houghton 14486.42.5. Houghton Library, Harvard University.

Siddons, Sarah. *The Reminiscences of Sarah Kemble Siddons 1773–1785.* Edited by William Van Lennep. Cambridge: Printed at Widener Library, 1942.

Smith, Bruce R. *The Acoustic World of Early Modern England: Attending to the O-Factor.* Chicago: University of Chicago Press, 1999.

Smith, Mark M. *Listening to Nineteenth-Century America.* Chapel Hill: University of North Carolina Press, 2000.

The Spouter's Companion; or, Theatrical Remembrancer. London: Printed for J. Cooke, 1770.

Staël, Germaine de. *Corinne, or Italy.* Translated by Avriel H. Goldberger. New Brunswick: Rutgers University Press, 1987.

Sterne, Jonathan. *The Audible Past: Cultural Origins of Sound Reproduction.* Durham: Duke University Press, 2003.

Stewart, Garrett. *Reading Voices: Literature and the Phonotext.* Berkeley: University of California Press, 1990.

Stocking, Marion Kingston, ed. *The Clairmont Correspondence: Letters of Claire Clairmont, Charles Clairmont, and Fanny Imlay Godwin.* 2 vols. Baltimore: Johns Hopkins University Press, 1995.

Stone, George Winchester, Jr., ed. *The London Stage 1660–1800.* Part 4, 1747–1776. Carbondale: Southern Illinois University Press, 1963.

Stone, George Winchester, Jr., ed. *The London Stage 1660–1800.* Part 5, 1776–1800. Carbondale: Southern Illinois University Press, 1964.

Strachey, Lytton. "Sarah Bernhardt." *Century Magazine* 106 (July 1923): 468–70.

Straub, Kristina. *Sexual Subjects: Eighteenth-Century Players and Sexual Ideology.* Princeton: Princeton University Press, 1992.

Taylor, John. *Records of My Life.* New York: J. and J. Harper, 1833.

"Theatrical Farewells. Garrick and Siddons." *Every Saturday* 4 (10 August 1867): 161–65.

Thomas, Downing A. "Architectural Visions of Lyric Theater and Spectatorship in Late-Eighteenth-Century France." *Representations* 52 (Fall 1995): 52–75.

Thomas, Russell. "Contemporary Taste in the Stage Decorations of London Theatres, 1770–1800." *Modern Philology* 42 (Nov. 1944): 65–78.

Thompson, Emily. *The Soundscape of Modernity: Architectural Acoustics and the Culture of Listening in America, 1900–1933.* Cambridge: MIT Press, 2002.

Vince, R. W. "Theatre History as an Academic Discipline." In *Interpreting the Theatrical Past: Essays in the Historiography of Performance*, edited by Thomas Postlewait and Bruce A. McConachie. Iowa City: University of Iowa Press, 1989. 1–18.

Walne, Graham. *Sound for Theaters: A Basic Manual.* Eastbourne, East Sussex: John Offord (Publications) Ltd., 1981.

Walpole, Horace. *Horace Walpole's Correspondence with the Countess of Ossory.* 3 vols. Edited by W. S. Lewis and A. Dayle Wallace. New Haven: Yale University Press, 1965.

Weiner, Stephanie Kuduk. "Listening with John Clare." *Studies in Romanticism* 48 (2009): 371–90.

West, Shearer. "Body Connoisseurship." In *Notorious Muse: The Actress in British Art and Culture, 1776–1812*, edited by Robyn Asleson. New Haven: Yale University Press, 2003. 151–70.

West, Shearer. "The Public and Private Roles of Sarah Siddons." In *A Passion for Performance: Sarah Siddons and Her Portraitists*, edited by Robyn Asleson. Los Angeles: The J. Paul Getty Museum, 1999. 1–40.

West, Shearer. "Siddons, Celebrity and Regality: Portraiture and the Ageing Actress." In *Theatre and Celebrity in Britain, 1660–2000*, edited by Mary Luckhurst and Jane Moody. New York: Palgrave Macmillan, 2005. 191–213.

Whitley, William Thomas. *Gainsborough.* New York: Charles Scribner's Sons, 1915.

Wolfson, Susan J., ed. *"Soundings of Things Done": The Poetry and Poetics of Sound in the Romantic Ear and Era.* Romantic Circles. Praxis Series. Available at http://www.rc.umd.edu/praxis/soundings/index.html.

Woo, Celestine. *Romantic Actors and Bardolatry: Performing Shakespeare from Garrick to Kean.* New York: Peter Lang, 2008.

Woo, Celestine. "Sarah Siddons as Hamlet: Three Decades, Five Towns, Absent Breeches, and Rife Critical Confusion." *ANQ* 20 (Winter 2007): 37–44.

Wood, Gillen D'Arcy. *The Shock of the Real: Romanticism and Visual Culture, 1760–1860.* New York: Palgrave, 2001.

Wood, James. "How Shakespeare's 'Irresponsibility' Saved Coleridge." In *The Irresponsible Self: On Laughter and the Novel.* New York: Picador, 2004. 42–58.

Wordsworth, William. *The Poetical Works of William Wordsworth.* 5 vols. Edited by Ernest de Selincourt and Helen Darbishire. Oxford: Clarendon Press, 1952–59.

Wordsworth, William. *William Wordsworth.* Edited by Stephen Gill. New York: Oxford University Press, 1984.

Worrall, David. *Theatric Revolution: Drama, Censorship and Romantic Period Subcultures 1773–1832.* Oxford: Oxford University Press, 2006.

Worthen, W. B., with Peter Holland, eds. *Theorizing Practice: Redefining Theatre History.* New York: Palgrave Macmillan, 2003.

Index

Printed and bound by CPI Group (UK) Ltd, Croydon, CR0 4YY